Michael took Grace's hand and kissed it.

She met his dark gaze with a searching one of her own, and her skin tingled where his lips touched. Fresh cheers rose from the crowd.

An usher stepped onto the stage and presented a huge bouquet of red roses and a gold foil package to Grace with a flourish.

Grace pulled out a music box of stained glass and caught her breath. She lifted the lid and the song "The Water Is Wide" spilled through her microphone and across the auditorium.

The tune chilled her with unwelcome memories.

An embossed gold card lay in the velvet lining. With carefully concealed reluctance, she pulled it out and scanned the childish scrawl on the elegant card. The chill in her spine intensified....

Books by Hannah Alexander

Love Inspired Suspense

*Note of Peril
*Under Suspicion
*Death Benefits
 Hidden Motive
 Season of Danger
  "Silent Night, Deadly Night"
 Eye of the Storm
 Collateral Damage

Love Inspired Historical

*Hideaway Home
 Keeping Faith

Steeple Hill Single Title

*Hideaway
*Safe Haven
*Last Resort
*Fair Warning
*Grave Risk
*Double Blind
 A Killing Frost
**Sacred Trust
**Solemn Oath
**Silent Pledge

*Hideaway novel
**Sacred Trust series

HANNAH ALEXANDER

is the pseudonym of husband-and-wife writing team Cheryl and Mel Hodde (pronounced "Hoddee"). When they first met, Mel had just begun his new job as an E.R. doctor in Cheryl's hometown, and Cheryl was working on a novel. Cheryl's matchmaking pastor set them up on an unexpected blind date at a local restaurant. Surprised by the sneak attack, Cheryl blurted the first thing that occurred to her, "You're a doctor? Could you help me paralyze someone?" Mel was shocked. "Only temporarily, of course," she explained when she saw his expression. "And only fictitiously. I'm writing a novel."

They began brainstorming immediately. Eighteen months later they were married, and the novels they set in fictitious Ozark towns began to sell. The first novel in the Hideaway series won the prestigious Christy Award for Best Romance in 2004.

NOTE OF PERIL
HANNAH ALEXANDER

HARLEQUIN® LOVE INSPIRED® SUSPENSE

In memory of our beloved aunt, Enid Larue Patterson,
born September 17, 1931, entered into rest October 24, 2004.
The legacy of her generous spirit will live on
in the hearts of the many people she has touched.

Recycling programs
for this product may
not exist in your area.

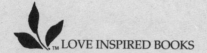

LOVE INSPIRED BOOKS

ISBN-13: 978-0-373-78868-2

Note of Peril

I will lie down and sleep in peace, for You alone,
O Lord, make me dwell in safety.
—*Psalms* 4:8

With special thanks to our friends
Stacy and April Frerking, our own Branson stars.
Thanks to their parents, Dennis and Bonnie,
for their loving friendship.

Thanks also to AJ the pharmacist for wonderful
poisoning ideas, to Jerry Ragsdale for insight into
the music world, and our brainstorming buddies,
Brenda Minton, Deborah Raney, Nancy Moser,
Judy Miller, Colleen Coble, Dave Coble,
Stephanie Whitson and Barbara Warren.

And Mom, once again, you're the best!

Chapter One

Colorful hues from multiple spotlights streaked across the stage in laser precision. The floor vibrated with the impact of drums as Grace Brennan smiled up at her Star Notes costar, Michael Gold.

"I saw you watching me from the corner of your eye," Michael sang, leaning forward and giving her a long, sultry look. "You like me, I can tell."

With an audacious wink at the audience, Grace placed a hand on Michael's chest and pushed him backward. "I know you think you saw something you did not see. I like my hound dog just as well."

As they continued their comedic duet, Grace felt a familiar tingle. Michael could sizzle the bark from a tree in January with those smoldering dark eyes. And his voice was on a par with Josh Groban's.

Three vocal backups—Cassidy Ryder, Delight Swenson and Blake Montana—joined them onstage, and the *Star Notes* show breezed on with all the energy and laughter of a typical night. The interactive show—like a country *Star Search*—had become so popular that the waiting list for guest amateur appearances was ridiculously long. The audition manager chose only the best vocalists, and the winner of each show was invited to return for further competition.

The theater was packed tonight due to the influx of tourists into Branson on the Friday after Thanksgiving. As the appreciative audience continued to applaud, Michael announced their final amateur guest vocalist of the evening. She came onstage and on cue began her ballad, with the *Star Notes* performers providing backup and harmony.

The *Star Notes* cast had intense practice sessions daily, and their expertise showed. They could make almost any voice sound good. The ongoing one-liners and repartee—which changed from night to night—kept the crowds coming back for more.

As the guest ended her song and turned to

leave the stage, Grace invited another round of applause.

Michael took Grace's hand and kissed it. She met his dark gaze with a searching one of her own, and her skin tingled where his lips touched. Fresh cheers rose from the crowd.

When the *Star Notes* director, Henry Bennett, had added romantic interaction to the show's script last year, the crowds had responded with enthusiasm. So had Michael. Only Grace continued to have misgivings about it. Sometimes she couldn't help wondering how much of what went on between her and Michael was an act, and how much was real. And lately she wondered about it after every performance.

As the applause died and the theater lights came on, Grace eagerly anticipated the final phase of the show. She loved talking with the audience.

An usher came down the aisle carrying a huge bouquet of red roses and a gold foil package. He stepped onto the stage and presented the items to Grace with a flourish. "Delivery services brought these for you, Miss Brennan."

The cast of the show often received flowers, gifts and cards from fans. Gifts brought onstage during the final few moments of the show added to the "reality" ambience—another of the director's ideas.

The card with the roses read "From your biggest fan," and it was signed "With love, Michael."

She read the note aloud, waited for the catcalls and applause to die down, then grinned up at Michael as he took the bouquet from her arms so she could open the lid of the package.

She pulled out a music box of stained glass and caught her breath. The jeweled colors reflected the stage lights with sparkling intensity in its artistic representation of a winding, whitecapped river.

"It's beautiful," she breathed, touching the box reverently. She looked up at Michael. "It's—"

But she caught him frowning at the gift, and saw the barely detectable shake of his head.

Okay, so this wasn't from him. She lifted the lid, and music from the song "The Water Is Wide" spilled across the auditorium as its notes were picked up by her microphone.

The tune chilled her with unwelcome memories.

A gold-embossed card lay on the velvet lining of the interior. With carefully concealed reluctance she pulled it out and scanned the childish scrawl on the elegant card. The chill in her spine intensified.

"Cheaters never prosper. Remember the contest? Soon everyone will know. There are some things time won't erase. And this is just the beginning."

Grace froze at the accusation. The chatter seemed to fade around her, and she grew intensely aware of the waiting audience.

She forced her smile back into place. No time to think about the ominous note now, or what lay behind it. She passed the gift to Delight, the youngest and most energetic member of the cast, who always welcomed a chance for the limelight.

Snap out of it, Grace. There'll be time to think about this later.

Michael frowned at the momentary look of shock in his costar's aquamarine eyes. Something was wrong. Just for a second, Grace's smile didn't quite fit.

The impression disappeared, but he studied her as she chatted with apparent spontaneity, charming her way into hearts as she always did—as she'd long ago done with him. Grace didn't realize the effect she had on people.

For the final set she had changed into a satin-and-lace gown in a rich dusky purple, and had caught her hair up in a rhinestone clip. Her face glowed with healthy color. She had been discovered by Henry in an amateur contest eight years ago. Henry had quickly recognized Grace's potential. Not only did she have a beautiful voice with exceptional range, but she was also a talented songwriter, whose words touched the very soul.

Michael doubted anyone else had noticed Grace's lapse of composure over the mystery gift. At last she thanked the audience for being there, and amid renewed applause made her way from the stage. Michael followed. Henry had called a meeting in the green room after the performance. They all knew the director would be waiting for them.

"Hey, Michael, you pulling some kind of prank?" called the band's drummer, Peter, as the rest of the cast filed along the wide hallway backstage.

Michael glanced over his shoulder at the man with spiky short hair and a hole in his ear—on Henry's stage, men weren't allowed to wear earrings or other jewelry that involved body piercing. "Prank?"

"What'd you do, ask her to marry you?" Blake Montana, the lead guitarist and bass backup, nudged Peter in the ribs.

Peter snickered. "Yeah, she looked sick."

Blake laughed, and the two jokers high-fived each other as Delight rolled her eyes at their juvenile humor.

Michael pulled off his cowboy hat as he glanced toward Grace, who walked alone several yards ahead of them. He knew she could hear the teasing, but she didn't respond or even turn around. Ordinarily she'd be bantering with the rest of them.

Michael excused himself, caught up with her and took her hand. "They think I sent the music box."

"I know you didn't," she said softly.

"So who did?" he asked.

"A secret enemy."

He glanced over his shoulder to make sure no one was listening. "I take it the card wasn't filled with good wishes."

"Definitely safe to say that."

He frowned. "Bad note?"

She nodded. "You can read it later."

"Who was it from?"

"I might tell you if I knew."

"Maybe a star wanna-be who didn't make the cut?"

She spread her free hand out to her side. "Everyone knows I don't choose who gets to join us onstage. The audition manager always makes a point of that with new contestants."

"But it's possible that a disgruntled person who didn't make the cut might take it out on you anyway."

They reached the open door to the green room, a large corner room spacious enough to accommodate all the performers. Michael touched Grace's arm and nodded in a silent gesture for her to wait for the others to enter first. He wanted a chance to talk to her a little longer.

Michael had met Grace backstage at the Roy Clark Theater when he worked as a stagehand and Grace as a backup vocalist. They discovered they shared the same hometown—Hideaway, Missouri, a village set on a peninsula on the shore of Table Rock Lake, much closer to Branson by boat than by the twisting, curving forest roads.

At the time of their first meeting, Michael had been testing the waters in the Branson music industry. Grace was hoping to build a career onstage, but for him, the theater was a rest from impending med school burnout and a chance to indulge in his love of music.

Now when Michael wasn't performing or practicing at the theater, he worked part-time as a phlebotomist and lab tech at Hideaway Clinic. He still loved medicine.

"So," Michael said when the last straggler had entered the room, leaving them alone in the hallway, "are you going to tell me what the card said?"

Just then the show's producer, Ladonna Macomb, stuck her head out the door and raised an eyebrow at them. "Henry's waiting."

"We're on our way," Grace said, then turned to Michael. "We'll talk later. I'm curious what's up with the boss."

Grace gave Michael a final, amused glance as he held the door for her to enter the green room. She could read frustration in the set of his jaw.

He trailed her to a table with two empty chairs and pulled one of them out for her as he hung his show hat on a hook on the wall. What gallantry. No wonder the man's telephone never stopped ringing and audiences cheered so enthusiastically when he stepped onto the stage.

Michael Gold was a gentleman, not to mention his proverbial tall, dark and handsome good looks. When Grace had first met Michael, he'd reminded her of Adam Cartwright from the television reruns of her mother's favorite show, *Bonanza.* She'd quickly learned that comments about his good looks embarrassed him, but he disguised his discomfort well in public with a casually amused attitude that served him well. And Michael didn't need to coast on his looks, for he was richly endowed with vocal talent.

His warm baritone voice could deepen to bass or climb the scales to high tenor.

Returning her thoughts to the present, Grace suddenly picked up on the tension in the room. Denton Mapes, the owner of the theater, sat on one of the sofas beside Delight, chatting softly to her. Most of the others had fallen silent. Henry sat in a chair at the table closest to the door, hooded eyes narrowed as he glared from person to person. Only Denton was spared the anger in the director's gaze.

Denton took a strong interest in the theater's activities, and tonight's visit was no surprise. The fact that he'd chosen to be seated beside a beautiful young woman was in character with his reputation as a ladies' man.

"We may be hitting the big time," Peter murmured to Cassidy, who sat across from him at the table next to Henry's. "How many other shows are sold out at this time of year?"

The director cleared his voice with pointed deliberation, glaring at Peter, then at the rest of them, his powerful bulldog jaw jutting forward. "Don't congratulate yourselves so quickly. You people seem to think that just because amateurs are brought onstage in your show, you can behave like amateurs, as well."

Silence blanketed the room, and Grace felt that old familiar tightening of her gut. Henry was in one of his moods—which was increasingly the case lately. His temper kept everyone on edge.

"How did we behave like amateurs?" Michael challenged.

Henry gestured toward Mitzi, the wardrobe manager, who sat to his left, shoulders slumped, gaze lowered as a flush crept up her slender neck and face. "I gave specific instructions about costumes for the first set, and Mitzi obviously didn't convey my message. She's been told that she'll be fired if it happens again."

Delight gasped.

"That wasn't her fault," Grace protested, bracing herself for the consequences but unable to remain silent. "I went into the wardrobe tonight and changed despite Mitzi's protests. No way was I going to wear that vulgar costume onstage."

"I didn't ask for your wardrobe advice," Henry snapped.

"This involved *my* wardrobe," Grace said firmly. "*Star Notes* isn't a peep show."

Delight barely stifled a laugh.

Henry redirected his irritated gaze at the sunny young blonde. "Are we entertaining you, Miss Swenson?"

She looked down at her hands and shook her head. "But I don't see what the big deal is. Like Grace always says, it's the music that counts, not the bare belly buttons. The guest vocalists just want the spotlight."

"You would do well to keep those lips together more often," Henry snapped.

The petite twenty-year-old blinked up at him. Grace noticed that Denton Mapes moved fractionally closer to Delight on the sofa, almost protectively.

"You're too new and too green to have any significant input." Henry continued to reprimand the young backup singer. "And no more ad-libbing with the harmony. You've got a long way to go before you have any kind of voice or stage presence."

Delight's fair complexion reddened as her gaze dropped once again to her hands.

Denton cleared his throat. "Henry, could we postpone this conference until our emotions are a little better controlled?"

Henry shot an irritable glance at the theater owner. "We have an agreement, in writing, that I'm the general partner. I'm in charge here, Mr. Mapes."

The director then transferred his brooding gaze to Grace. "I have an idea for you, Grace. Why don't you and Delight trade some secrets? She can show you how to lose weight and dress so you won't be ashamed to show that belly button, and you can teach her how to sing."

"Henry," Michael snapped, "that's enough!"

Stunned silence once more filled the room as heat rushed over Grace's face. If the ceiling had fallen at that moment, she would have been relieved. She'd long ago grown accustomed to Henry's blunt comments when he critiqued her performance in private, but this wasn't private. And he'd never been so caustic. Grace shot a glance at the other target of Henry's barbs. From Delight's look of misery, it appeared she shared Grace's sense of humiliation.

"Major bucks depend on your behavior," Henry said, rising to his feet and stalking through the room. "When you people mess up, we lose money, and when money is lost, *I'm* held responsible."

"We're making more money than ever before," Michael said. "As for costumes, I can't remember a time when you've ever disregarded a cast member's personal convictions."

The color in Henry's face deepened alarmingly, and his breathing came in short bursts.

"You need to take a moment to cool off," Michael warned.

"I'm fine," Henry snapped. He stopped in front of Grace. "Get the weight off." He switched the focus of his glare to Cassidy, the blond backup tenor with movie-star good looks. "And Ryder—or whatever you're calling yourself these days—there's far too much talk about your lady-killing ways lately, and that can hurt ratings."

"That isn't my fault," Cassidy said. "I can't help it if Jolene won't get her facts straight in that gossip column of hers. You know she makes up half the things she prints."

"Then don't even give her a reason to write about you," Henry snapped. "And practice smiling. Half the time you look like you're snarling onstage."

One more time the director turned his attention to Grace. "I've worked long and hard to put you where you are, Grace. Now you dare to throw it back in my face by refusing my orders on wardrobe?"

She stared at him helplessly. The man was out of control. Michael and Henry had been friends for several years. If Michael couldn't talk some sense into the director, no one else in this room had a chance.

"I want you to start listening to me, and trust that I know what I'm doing," Henry said, then pivoted and stalked to the door. "Time to go home." Without another word he walked out.

Chapter Two

Henry's words seemed to echo through the room as Delight stared at Denton Mapes's hand on her arm. She wanted to snatch it away and tell him to keep his hands to himself. Did he think he had a right to paw her just because he owned this theater?

She felt like telling Denton and Henry and Ladonna exactly where they could shove this theater. But that would be stupid. She desperately needed to make them happy, and time for that was running out.

Denton withdrew his hand. "Why don't we have a talk?"

"Nothing's stopping you." She knew she sounded like a sullen brat, but she felt like pouting for a few minutes.

"I think this conversation should be held

in a nice restaurant with soothing music and good food."

She gave him a suspicious look. *Soothing music?* What did he mean by that? Was he asking her for a date?

Denton was at least forty-five, with graying hair, bushy dark eyebrows and a face that looked as if he'd hit the bottle a few too many times. Or a bottle had hit him. He also had the reputation of using and losing women at breakneck speed.

Or wait…maybe this invitation had nothing to do with a lusting older man. *Soothing music.* Maybe she was about to be let go from the show. Why else would she need to be soothed?

Denton couldn't do that, could he? Just take her out to dinner and dump her from the show? He didn't strike her as the kind of man who would do Henry Bennett's dirty work.

"Where did you want to go?" she asked, surprised she even had a voice left.

Those thick eyebrows rose, as if he hadn't expected her to be interested. "How about Top of the Rock, near Big Cedar? I could reserve a table with a good view of the sunset."

Oh, sure. She wanted to watch the sunset with this boozer—this rich old boozer—while her career went down the drain. Very appetizing.

"The only time we could do that is on Monday," she said, "since I've got a show every other night."

"That works." He sounded almost eager. "Why don't I pick you up at your condo about five Monday evening?"

She studied his face. He didn't hold her gaze, but at least he didn't stare at other parts of her anatomy. Instead, his attention dropped to the floor, as if he was deep in thought about something else.

"You know where I live?" she asked.

He nodded, returning his attention to her.

She hesitated. Did she really want to do this?

But it wasn't as if Denton Mapes was some kind of rapist or killer. He owned this theater. "Fine, Mr. Mapes. See you then."

Grace rushed down the hallway, praying no one would approach her. Cassidy, Peter and Blake stood huddled by the vending machines, and only Cassidy glanced her way as she swept past them. She made eye contact with him briefly. Obviously the others had been as upset as she was by Henry's behavior.

She stormed into her dressing room, barely refrained from slamming the door behind her and glared at her reflection in the mirror. Okay, so she did have a little extra puffiness around her eyes lately. And her dresses all fit a little too snugly. But how much did that matter to the show?

She saw Michael's image in the mirror half a second before he spoke from the open doorway. "There should be speed limits in those hallways," he said as he entered the room. "What's the rush?"

She slumped onto her bench without turning around. Her humiliation was complete.

"Grace, he was way out of line."

She nodded. "Thanks for defending me."

"You stood up for Mitzi, and for your personal convictions. I'm proud of you."

She unfastened her rhinestone necklace and placed it carefully on the jewelry stand, noticing he hadn't given her a word of reassurance about Henry's diatribe. "And?"

He frowned at her. "And I'm afraid he might have given Delight a major shock."

"And what else struck you about the meeting, besides the fact that Henry was behaving like a jerk?"

He considered that question as his frown

deepened. "His anger was out of control, which probably has something to do with his blood sugar, but I didn't dare ask him about it after the meeting. He's headed for trouble if this stress continues."

Grace relented for a moment. Michael was right. Henry's health *had* deteriorated these past two years. His failing ability to control his emotional outbursts was a symptom of his physical condition.

Still, his words had plunged deeply and scraped bone.

"Could you persuade him to have a physical?" she asked.

"I'll have a talk with him after he's had a chance to calm down." Michael stepped up behind her at the dresser and placed his hands on her shoulders. "Are you okay?"

"Oh, sure. I love it when the director castigates me for being fat. It's an especially sweet experience in front of an audience." *Especially when no one contradicts him.*

"He overdid it a bit, didn't he?"

She stiffened. *A bit?* "*You* think I'm too fat?"

He pulled out a chair and sank into it beside her. "Nope, I think you're just fat enough."

She smacked him on the arm and he

laughed, grabbing her hand to keep her from hitting him again.

"Do you ever take anything seriously?" she asked as she pulled away.

"Sure I do. Fishing. My horse. Riding my Harley."

She swiveled her chair away from her reflection in the mirror. Michael had a knack for drawing her out of herself, and right now she really appreciated that. "What about God?"

He paused, then winked at her. "You've got me there. Definitely God is to be taken seriously, but I don't think He's just sitting up on a cloud somewhere watching us, ready to tromp on us every time we blow it. Mind telling me why the sudden change of subject?"

She gestured toward the beautiful stained-glass music box on her dresser. "I'm sorry. I can't get that out of my mind."

He frowned and leaned closer. "God has something to do with the gift you received tonight?"

She allowed herself to be lost in those dark brown eyes for about half a second, then she reached for the box and raised the lid. The familiar tinkling song spiraled through the room as she picked up the card and handed it to Michael. She closed the lid quickly to shut off the music.

He read the inscription, then handed it back to her. "What's going on? Who's a cheater, and what contest is this referring to?"

She took the card and slid it back beneath the stained-glass lid without setting off the music again. "About three years before I met you, I entered a music contest sponsored by Henry and some of his business associates."

"That would have been eight years ago."

She rested her elbows on the dresser and rubbed her eyes wearily, not caring that it would probably smudge her makeup. "I sang that song for the contest." She gestured toward the music box. "I didn't realize until later that they preferred original songs."

"And you won anyway?" he guessed.

She nodded. "And unfortunately, I *was* aware that the contest was for amateurs. No one was eligible who had already earned more than five hundred dollars from their music. I had earned more than that singing with a band at some concerts in the four-state area."

"So you were young and you blew it. What did Henry do when you told him?"

"What makes you think I told him?"

"I know you."

"It gets messier," she said. "I heard later that the other judges had chosen another contestant, and Henry had done some major cajoling to change the results. Seems I wasn't the only one who cheated. The winner had bought off the judges."

"Anyone you knew?"

"Nope. The contestants never met. I heard later the guy's name was Wes Reinhold, but he's never been heard of around here since. Apparently Wes went ballistic and threatened Henry. Not a smart thing to do. Henry's always had a lot of contacts among the major players in this town. Wes had the sense to move on."

"So what happened then?" Michael asked.

"A few months later I had a 'come to Jesus' moment. Literally. I embraced the faith my mother had tried so hard to instill in me, and I went to Henry and told him about my lie."

"Did he care?"

She shrugged. "He said it was too late to do anything about it, and that I had a promising career ahead of me. I didn't know what else to do, so I just let it go."

Michael glanced at the music box with a frown, leaning forward with elbows on his knees. "After all this time, why is someone suddenly making a big deal about it?"

"Could be they're just finding out."

"You don't think it could be this Wes guy, could it?"

Grace shrugged. "He could easily have discovered I misrepresented my amateur status, since the music community is so closely woven here in Branson, but as I said, he moved on."

"People don't always stay gone," Michael said. "Still, I think this whole thing began and ended tonight. Someone discovered that past mistake and decided to chide you a little. But you mentioned God. Where does He come into this?"

"If my name is discredited, then so is the God I serve."

"My dad always warned me not to borrow trouble," Michael said, "and he knew what he was talking about. He had me. He didn't have to *borrow* trouble."

Grace cast her gaze to the ceiling, but she couldn't resist a smile. "I rest my case. You never do get serious."

"All things in moderation, as Dad always said. You know, if you're really worried, you could go public with the news," he said quietly. "Beat your note-passer to the punch."

Grace struggled with the clasp on the bracelet that matched her necklace. "Maybe."

Michael pushed her fingers away and reached for the clasp, unfastened it and placed it on the jewelry stand with the matching necklace.

He had a healing touch. He also had a healing voice. When Grace listened to him sing during practice, she could feel her whole body relax.

Grace knew Michael's laid-back attitude wasn't the result of never suffering pain or loss. His mother had died when he was ten. His father—a minister—had passed on when Michael was seventeen, leaving Michael with major debt. When he was in his third year of med school, his aunt—his final close relative—passed away. In the aftermath, Michael had quit school.

"Written any songs lately?" he asked.

"A couple. You?"

"One or two."

"Any serious ones?" she teased. Michael had a knack for humor, and he particularly liked songs that pertained to children or romance—even if the romance was between a couple of broken-down old horses in his neighbor's pasture.

"Life's too serious as it is," he said.

"The women go wild over a big, handsome, broody hunk like you who sings about kids and love."

Instead of blushing, as she'd expected, he caught her gaze and held it. No smile. "I'm not interested in a bunch of women going wild over me. Just one woman."

"Of course," she said with a grin. "That's why they love you. A one-woman man who hasn't found his woman yet."

"They all know better," he said, then sighed and leaned back, fiddling with the rim of the cowboy hat he'd worn onstage. "You're the one with the writing talent. When you sing 'Daddy, Don't,' I doubt there's a dry eye in the theater. That one digs deep."

She rested her elbows on the dresser. "Thank you. It's autobiographical."

He didn't even blink. "I always wondered about your father. Neither you nor your mom ever talk about him."

She studied Michael's earnest face for a moment. "The last time I saw him, the police were hauling him out the door after he'd beaten me nearly senseless."

Compassion shone in Michael's eyes. "What happened?"

"I was sixteen. I'd come home late one night from a music recital. He was drinking, he got mad, I mouthed off and he went after me. Mom tried to stop him, and he punched her in the stomach. Hard."

Michael winced. "I'm sorry."

"We left him out in California—in prison— and moved to Hideaway."

"You never told me about that."

"It isn't something a person goes around talking about," she said. "It left some scars."

"What kinds of scars?" Michael asked gently.

"For instance, whenever I get really tired or the weather changes, I walk with a limp because of some damage I took that night."

"Your mother never thought about leaving him before that happened?"

Grace kicked off her shoes. Enough soul baring for one night. "Nope. She doesn't believe in divorce. As long as he picked on her and not me, she stuck it out. Now, are you going to get out of here so I can change clothes?"

He slowly rose from his chair, reached

out and gave a wayward strand of her hair a gentle tug, then left the room, closing the door behind him.

The main women's dressing room coldly reflected the overheads from the long mirror. Everyone else had left. Delight picked up a hairbrush from the counter and raised it to her head.

The bristles scratched her forehead. She winced and hurled the brush across the room. It smacked against the far wall with a thwack as she sank onto a bench and burst into tears.

"No stage presence, Delight Swenson." She mimicked Henry's guttural growl. "You should have Grace teach you how to do it. Grace is a goddess. Grace can walk on water. Grace, Grace, Grace."

"Hello in there." Blake Montana's deep voice sounded from the doorway.

"Goodbye," she called back.

"You decent?"

"Never."

There was a snicker. "Okay, well, did I hear you kick something, or did the ceiling fall on someone named Grace?"

She grimaced and raked the back of her

hand across the moisture on her face. "I'm not up to company."

Blake entered in spite of her protest, his tall frame filling the doorway. "You been crying?"

"Go away." She wasn't in the mood to talk. She swung around and grabbed her sable coat from the rack beside the dressing-room door. She would wear this gown home tonight, and Mitzi could worry about it later.

She stalked past Blake out of the dressing room, not bothering to close the door behind her. Blake did it for her, then caught up with her in seconds.

"I don't need an escort," she snapped.

"Mind if I walk you out to the car anyway?" he asked. "I'm parked beside you, and it's dark out there. In your frame of mind, no one would dare attempt to mug us."

She glared at him over her shoulder. No way was he going to tease her out of this bad mood. She'd earned it.

Blake Montana had light brown hair that reached his shoulders, and the indentation of his show hat was visible around the crown of his head. He had sincerely kind eyes the color of chocolate toffee, a good, strong bass voice, and he could work magic with a guitar, a fiddle and a harmonica.

He leaned forward and inspected her face. "Your eyes are all puffy, but it doesn't look like a case of Cassidy's allergies to me."

"I don't know what you're talking about."

"That guy has so many allergies, if a cat walked across the stage tomorrow night, Cassidy'd probably fall over dead. Did you know he carries an epi pen around with him all the time? He has to, in case he has a bad reaction to something."

She shoved the cast entrance door open before Blake could beat her to it. Knowing Cassidy Ryder, allergies were the least of his problems. He had an ego the size of Alaska, and he fit right in with a bushel of other hungry wanna-be stars.

"The guy's always nervous," Blake continued. "He's pretty high-strung."

Delight snorted. High-strung? Was that what they called delusions of grandeur?

"Did you know your makeup's smeared all over your face?"

"Well, I'm sure Grace's makeup isn't smudged," she snapped. "It's probably perfect. Grace is perfect. Why don't you go bother her?"

"Grace?" Blake exclaimed. "I thought you two were buds."

"I'm her flunky, just there to make her look good. And sound good. And suck up whenever I can so she'll feel special. After all, *she's* the star."

Blake didn't reply, and Delight realized how much resentment had spilled into her words. She didn't care. She'd warned him to leave her alone.

Until tonight, Delight had idolized Grace. But when Henry made those nasty remarks, something inside had snapped. The man treated Grace like a favorite niece even when he was chewing her out. *He treats me like an unwanted dog.*

Blake followed Delight to her car and waited while she unlocked and opened the door. "You're not the only person who says things she doesn't mean when she's mad, Delight."

"Can it," she snapped. "I don't want a sermon."

"Don't let Henry's words bother you so much. You make those amateur singers sound like a choir of angels."

Delight hesitated and looked up at him. Did

he really think that, or was he just trying to make her feel better?

"Get over it, Delight. Shake it off and go on. You're more mature than this."

She scowled. "You're saying I'm behaving like a kid?"

"I'm just saying don't let tonight break you," Blake said. "You can rise above it."

"I'll rise above it, all right," she said, shutting the door on him. "I'll beat Henry at his own game."

Chapter Three

On Monday morning Grace awakened to the jarring chirp of her cell phone beside the bed. As she burrowed from under the covers and reached for it, she accidentally knocked it to the floor.

Last night, after the Sunday-evening show, she'd had the sudden urge to get out of Branson for a while, so instead of going back to her condo in town, she'd driven home to Hideaway. Sundays were especially tiring when they did two shows.

She retrieved her cell phone from the floor and glanced at the tiny display panel. Her agent's number flashed at her, and she opened the flip top.

"It's about time." The husky voice of Sherilyn Krueger came over the line.

"I guess you know this is my day off," Grace groused.

"Where are you?"

"Who wants to know?"

"You're obviously not home. I tried calling four times, and all I got was your recorder."

"Did you ever consider just leaving a message? And I *am* home. I'm in Hideaway."

"Aha! Who'd you go to see?" There was a teasing tone to Sherilyn's voice.

Grace curled her lip at the phone. "I came to be home. Period. In my old apartment, above my mom's antique store." Since when did an agent have the right to pry into a client's personal life?

"Oh." Exaggerated disappointment curled through the phone line. "If you had any brains, you'd make the most of your opportunity with that gorgeous costar of yours."

Grace scowled. Sherilyn was an in-your-face lady with the charm of a collie and the tenacity of Bertie Meyer's pet goat, Mildred. Henry had bullied Grace into signing on with Sherilyn years ago. It was a good match. Usually.

Grace peered at her bedside clock. "Sherilyn, it isn't even eight. I came here to get *away* from work."

"It's the beginning of a new week," Sherilyn said. "Perfect time for you to start your new diet, and it sounds as if I've caught you before breakfast."

Grace shoved the covers back. "Not this morning. I've got a date with waffles and an old friend." She missed Bertie Meyer almost as much as she did her own mother.

At the extended silence on the other end of the line, Grace frowned. Sherilyn's comment about diet suddenly registered. "Okay, who's been talking to you about Friday night's meeting?"

"What do you mean, talk? All I had to do was open the magazine and read all about it. Right there on the second page of *Across the Country,* pictures and all, especially you in that suede gunnysack you call a dress."

"You can't believe what they print. Jolene Tucker distorts the facts beyond imagination."

"Honey, you're changing the subject. You and me are going 'round and 'round about this weight problem until you get it licked," Sherilyn said. "No pun intended. I want you in shape for Christmas."

Grace leaned back against the headboard and groaned. "Did I mention this is my only day off?"

"Did it occur to you that I don't give a rip about your days off?" Sherilyn drawled. "I work 24/7 for you, and I need you in top form. Tell you what, I'll read this article to you if you want, word for word, and if that don't make you lose your appetite, honey, then nothing—"

"Don't bother. I'm changing my cell phone number."

There was a dark chuckle. "I'll just show up on your doorstep."

"Who leaked the meeting to Jolene?"

"I don't know, and it doesn't matter," Sherilyn said. "We'll turn those lemons into lemonade. This morning all you get for breakfast is eggs and Canadian bacon or lean ham. No bread, no fruit, no pancakes."

"Sorry, but I plan to have black walnut waffles for breakfast this morning." Bertie Meyer was famous for them. To drive to Hideaway and not have Bertie's waffles was almost heresy around these parts.

"You don't want me hunting you down," Sherilyn warned.

In spite of her irritation, Grace couldn't resist a smile. "You can join me if you want."

"Unlike some folks, I've got work to do.

Now, about that magazine article," Sherilyn said. "Do you have a copy?"

Grace knew her mother read those gossip magazines faithfully, cutting out any articles that mentioned Grace's name or the show. There would be a copy of it around at the house somewhere. "Okay, I'll stick with the diet for today."

"That's a start. Hurry back to town. I've got a present for you."

"What's that?"

"A gift membership to a health club."

"Don't you have other clients to harass?"

"None as important to me as you are. Give me a month—we'll get you into better shape. Meanwhile, I'll be stalking you." She hung up before Grace could argue further.

Michael parked his Harley in the sunshine outside the Classical Impressions Theater, just east of the Branson Medows Mall. He was chilled to the bone.

Why hadn't he driven his Mountaineer, like any sane person would have done?

He lingered in the sun for a moment, hoping the heat would seep through the black leather of his jacket. It was an unseasonably warm day for late November, and tour-

ists crowded the streets and sidewalks. He'd
counted eight tour buses on Highway 76 as
he'd driven to town. It was still nothing like
what they experienced during high season,
but colder months were increasingly becoming attractive to tourists. So far this week
they'd sold out shows three nights in a row.

Henry's sleek black Mercedes was parked
next to the cast entrance of the theater. Besides that, only a couple of other cars—in-
cluding Delight's Dodge Viper—graced the
lot. Michael hadn't seen this place so quiet
in a while.

He unzipped his jacket and carried his helmet inside, where he paused to allow time
for his eyes to adjust to the dimness after the
bright light outside.

He found the director upstairs in his office,
which overlooked the auditorium and stage.
Any time Henry saw something he didn't like
during practice, he simply slid open the window and shouted his orders to those onstage.

In spite of Henry's occasionally caustic
persona, Michael admired the man's passion for producing excellent musical entertainment. Lately, though, his mind seemed
to be slipping.

Michael knocked on the threshold of the open door.

Henry peered over his reading glasses. "Wondered when you'd show up." His bull-dog face showed resignation.

"Hi, Henry."

"Come on in, sit down. You look set on a lecture." The silver-haired man leaned back in his luxurious executive chair and removed his glasses, frowning at the black leather and the helmet under Michael's left arm. "You biked to town?"

Michael set down his helmet and pulled off his jacket. Though he hadn't thawed out yet, he knew he soon would. This room was always hotter by ten degrees than any other place in the theater. "I didn't come here to lecture you."

Henry snorted. "I saw your face the other night when I lit into Grace. Struck a little too close to home, did I?"

Michael pretended he hadn't heard the gibe. "When did you have your last medi-cal checkup?" He sank into the chair closest to the desk, for once grateful for the heated room.

"A couple of months ago, maybe three."

"I brought my stethoscope and blood pressure kit."

Henry closed his eyes and produced a long-suffering sigh. "You're not playing doctor again, are you?"

"Don't hurt my feelings." On good days Henry Bennett reminded Michael of his dad. Michael still missed his father's quiet strength and encouragement.

"First we need to clear the air," Henry said.

"Okay. You were mean Friday night."

Henry fixed his steely-blue gaze on Michael, then glanced toward the door. "Anybody come with you?"

"You're kidding, right? You think someone else is nuts enough to ride on my Harley with me all the way here just to face down the bear in his cave?"

Henry pulled open the top drawer of his desk. "Funny, I thought I heard someone else down there a few minutes ago."

"I saw Delight's car in the lot."

Henry scowled. "Humor me, then, and close the door."

As Michael meekly obeyed, Henry pulled out his glucose monitoring kit and pricked his finger. He pressed the droplet of blood onto a strip, waited a moment, then nodded in satisfaction. "It's been fluctuating lately. I'm keeping a closer eye on it, so you can relax, Doc."

"When's the last time you checked your blood pressure?"

"I said relax. I do that a couple of times a week with my own kit. Now, to clear the air," Henry said, leaning forward, "I'll apologize to Grace for being so rough on her Friday."

"And she'll forgive you, even though our supposedly private conversation did get leaked to the press."

Henry nodded gravely. "I didn't mean for that to happen. Ironically, I think it'll just whet the public's appetite. Did you see the column?"

"Nope, but I heard a few remarks about it this morning over breakfast in Hideaway," Michael said.

Henry paused and glanced toward the door again. "Enough about that. This is confidential, Michael. Promise me you won't share this with anyone but Grace. Not even your horse."

"That's asking a lot. I tell my horse everything."

Henry barely broke a grin. "I had a video cut of the show Friday night." He clasped his hands behind his head and swiveled in his chair to gaze out across the darkened theater. "I sent it to a country music cable network. They're thinking about scheduling *Star Notes* next year."

Michael could hear the sudden excitement in Henry's voice, and saw it on his face. "Television?"

"That's right." Henry turned back to look at him. "It's been my dream for fifteen years to have a television production. You and Grace are talented enough to make it happen, Michael. Unfortunately, Denton's pushing for changes, and even though I'm general partner, he's got clout."

"You should have remembered that the other night. You weren't exactly polite to him."

Henry frowned, nodding in agreement. "He could make some waves with the other partners."

"What changes is he wanting?" Michael asked.

"He wants to cut back on Grace's songs. He's asking for fewer spiritual pieces."

Michael stiffened. "Her songs make up more than half our music. Doesn't Denton get it? She's the major draw."

Henry gave an irritable shrug. "Sometimes

we have to compromise. He wants to continue doing original music, but include pieces from another new writer he's discovered. Denton's the one complaining about Grace's weight and wardrobe, by the way." He closed his eyes. "He wants Delight to receive more spotlight time."

"Delight? That's why you blasted her so hard Friday?"

"Partly that, and partly because she irritates me to death. She's a loose cannon. Too young to handle success."

"She also can't bring in the crowds Grace draws," Michael said. Grace had come into her own on this show. Wasn't that obvious to everyone concerned?

Henry rubbed his lined face, which showed the recent effects of long hours at the theater. "Denton has a lot of contacts with the television people. He could be our ticket to a broader audience than any of us have ever had before, and that could mean substantially more income for all of us."

"It doesn't sound as if the audience he has in mind is the one we're accustomed to."

Henry reached for a folder filled with sheet music and shoved it across the desk. "He's been pushing me to include some of these on the show. Read the top song."

Michael read the first few lines and realized the song wouldn't work for them. The lyrics left nothing to the imagination. The words didn't just imply a relationship between the singers—they spoke of it in overtly sexual tones.

He slid the pages back into the folder. "You know Grace and I couldn't do this."

"Denton suggested Delight and Cassidy."

A quiet bump, like a footfall, reached Michael from the hallway. He glanced toward the door, but heard nothing else. He turned back to Henry. "Don't become so desperate for a television show that you lose sight of what we're about."

"No problem there," the director said dryly. "I'll always have you to remind me."

Delight stood in the hallway outside Henry's office and stifled a gasp of shock. *Television!* She felt as if her feet had suddenly been glued to the carpet, and as desperately as she wanted to walk away before someone caught her and accused her of eavesdropping—which she was *not*—she couldn't move.

Who else was in there besides Michael and

Henry? In spite of her pounding heart, she leaned closer to the door.

"Our fans are conservative and expect a wholesome quality from the show," Michael said. "They're the ones who would look for us on television. Denton's plans threaten to destroy everything we stand for."

Delight had to breathe slowly and deeply to keep from hyperventilating. They really were talking about *Star Notes* making television!

"What about this one?" came Henry's voice. "Nothing lewd or suggestive, just a simple country 'you done me wrong with another man' song."

Heart pounding so loudly she could barely hear the voices, Delight turned to leave.

"I want you and Grace to sing it, not Cassidy and Delight," Henry said. "We can keep damage to a minimum."

Delight stopped and turned back. That old buzzard had always hated her, but why was he suddenly so nasty? As far as she could remember, she'd never done anything mean to him.

"Look, I'm willing to work with you, Henry," Michael said. "Grace and I both know this isn't a gospel show, and that we're just performers, not partners. I'll talk to her if you'll let me take this with me."

"Do whatever you can to remain in Denton's good graces," Henry said. "Meanwhile I'm going to make sure Delight stays out of the picture as much as possible."

"Don't be too hard on her," Michael said. "She's young and energetic, and she adds vibrancy to the show. She needs some room to make mistakes."

"She can make mistakes on her own time."

Delight glared at the door, fists clenching so tightly her fingernails dug in to the soft flesh of her palms. That arrogant old blowhard! Why did he hate her so much?

The door opened as she stood there gaping, and her future flashed before her eyes. In agony she watched her career die a horrible death.

Michael hovered in the doorway, frowning. Henry glared at her from his desk.

"May we help you?" Michael asked. His voice was gentle, but filled with an unspoken question.

For several seconds, frozen with mortification, she couldn't say anything. *Suck it up, Delight. They're watching.* "I was lookin' for Den—uh, Mr. Mapes." She swallowed through a suddenly dry throat. "I tried callin' him from home, but his number's unlisted, and I need to...um...is he around?"

"No, he's not," Henry snapped. "You shouldn't be, either."

She gritted her teeth. "I wasn't—"

"Get out of here, you two," Henry muttered. "I'm busy."

Delight pivoted and rushed down the hallway. Her face burned with painful humiliation as tears stung her eyes. All she'd wanted to do was find Denton and call off the date for tonight, but would Henry ever believe she hadn't been deliberately spying? Of course not. He was a black-hearted old—

"Delight?"

She ignored Michael's voice behind her. How many times had she wished she could talk to him alone, away from Grace and the rest of the cast? But this wasn't what she'd had in mind.

A touch on her arm startled her, and she jerked around and looked up into mesmerizing dark brown eyes that could boil water with their intensity. She caught her breath.

"I really wasn't eavesdropping," she said. "Not intentionally, anyway. I don't care what Henry says."

"Don't take Henry's words to heart right now. If you heard anything at all, you know he's under a lot of pressure."

"He hates me."

"See? There you go, taking it personally."

She warmed to the teasing tone of Michael's voice and fell into step beside him. What she wouldn't give to be his costar. Grace didn't even realize what she had.

"I don't know what I've done to Henry," she said, "but it's obvious how he feels about me."

"Give him time. He was that hard on me once, years ago. On Grace, too, for that matter."

"How long before that changed?"

"I worked with him for the first time six years ago. I just did a brief substitution for another musician, but we remained friends afterward. He remembered me when he was putting the cast together for *Star Notes*. He also insisted Grace and I work together."

"Well, he'd never try to boost *my* career."

"You're looking at it the wrong way. He wants what's best for the show. Right now, that's Grace. You're what, twenty? You've got lots of time."

"I don't see what age has to do with it."

"Experience has everything to do with it. Grace has ten years on you. Just settle in and pay your dues."

Delight wanted to scowl. Instead, she poked Michael in the side with her fingers and grinned up at him. "So, you think I'm young and energetic."

He laughed as they reached the broad staircase that led downstairs to the lobby. "Don't take that personally, either."

She stopped and allowed him to take the stairs without her. "Hey! What's that supposed to mean?"

"It means you have a lot of potential, and you have time to develop it." He glanced up at her over his shoulder. "Give it the time it needs, and mature into it."

The words struck her like a slap. In other words, he was telling her to grow up. First Blake, now Michael.

Stinging from the rebuke, she watched Michael reach the lobby and cross to the cast entrance. With a casual wave over his shoulder, he walked out.

Chapter Four

Michael's cell phone vibrated in his shirt pocket just before he pulled his helmet on, bracing himself for a chilly ride home. As he retrieved the phone from his pocket, he caught sight of Delight striding from the cast entrance, hands stuffed deeply into the pockets of her fur coat.

"Hey, gorgeous." A familiar husky voice came from the phone.

"Hi, Sherilyn." Grace's determined agent had wooed him professionally for months now, in spite of his rejections.

"Had lunch yet?" she asked.

"I slept late, had a late breakfast."

She tsked him. "You and Grace Brennan are like two nuts from the same tree. Fortunately for her, I'm curbing her breakfast choices for a while, which will be difficult for her down at Bertie's."

"She's in Hideaway today?" With a pang he realized he'd missed her.

"That's right, and she'd better be sticking to my diet plan. You didn't happen to catch the article in yesterday's *Across the Country,* did you?"

Delight peeled out of the parking lot in her Viper, and Michael looked up to see her barely missing a car in traffic. "I avoid that magazine whenever possible, though I've heard about the article."

The last time his face had been plastered across the pages of that magazine the headline had read Heartthrob Branson Singer Michael Gold Pulled Over For Drunk Driving. The reporter hadn't bothered to explain that the patrolman discovered Michael had not been drinking, but had been distracted by a stray puppy sauntering into the street.

"I advise you to snatch a copy from the closest newsstand," Sherilyn said. "Jolene was rough on Grace this time. Made a big deal about the meeting Friday night."

"I heard."

"I've got a radio station looking for a guest celebrity for an upcoming Saturday segment."

The sudden change in subject was typical Sherilyn. "Preferably male. Interested?"

He chuckled, enjoying the warmth of the sunshine as it heated him through the black leather of his jacket. "My Saturdays are tied up."

"It wouldn't interfere with practice, because it's Saturday morning. It'd bring some good publicity your way for a change."

"Sorry, I'll have to pass." He wasn't about to give up his Saturday-morning work at the clinic to build a music career he'd suddenly begun to have doubts about.

She sighed audibly. "You do play hard to get, Michael Gold. I could do your career a world of good, you know."

"I'm sure you could." He occasionally caught himself cringing lately when he saw a photo of himself in the media. "How about Cassidy Ryder? He's a celebrity."

Sherilyn gave an unladylike snort over the phone. "You're the one I want."

He chuckled and said goodbye, then zipped up his jacket and braced himself for a cool ride—maybe he could make it back home in thirty minutes if he took an alternate route out of town.

* * *

Grace sat on the sun-drenched deck of the Lakeside Bed and Breakfast, ignoring strange looks from the lunch crowd inside the dining area as she read the final lines of the article Sherilyn had been so insistent that she read.

Finished, she shoved the magazine across the table in disgust. She wanted to throw it into the water, but that would be littering. Besides, it was her mom's copy.

"'Overly voluptuous,'" she muttered, leaning back in her chair and staring across the water toward the opposite shore.

The screen door opened, and Bertie Meyer stepped onto the deck carrying a large bowl of greens and chopped veggies topped with slices of grilled chicken. "This oughta fill you up, gal. At least for a couple of hours."

The wily white-haired octogenarian set the bowl down. "Won't help to brood."

"You read the article?"

"Sure I did. Half the folks in town read it. We keep up with your career, you know. We're all so proud of our hometown boy and girl making good." Bertie sat down across the table from Grace with a groan of relief.

"You call that *good?*" Grace gestured at the magazine.

"I call it dirty. I'd like to get hold of the person who wrote it and teach her some manners. Still, they wouldn't be writing that stuff about you if you weren't in the public eye. And the reason you're in the public eye is because they love you."

Grace shook her head and managed a smile, remembering why she'd always adored Bertie.

The older lady gestured to the salad. "That's one of the recipes I fixed up for Karah Lee over at the clinic. Grilled chicken salad with salsa. Says she's lost thirty pounds and still going at it."

Grace studied the salad. Karah Lee was the tall, beautiful, outspoken redheaded doctor who dated Ranger Jackson Taylor. Come to think of it, she *had* lost some weight lately.

"How'd you like that breakfast I made you this morning?" Bertie asked.

"Delicious. Was that one of Karah Lee's recipes, too?"

"Yep."

After saying a blessing over her food, Grace ate with a relish that surprised her. If the diet continued to be this good, she might be able to live with it.

Bertie glanced through the plate-glass window into the interior dining room. "Looks like customers are clearing out."

Grace nodded. Most of the fall and winter crowd were antique hunters, retirees with lots of time and a little money on their hands. As they left the lodge, they'd be headed back to the serious business of searching for their next bargain.

Her mom's shop, Vintage Treasures, was one of the most popular in town. Her mom's assistant, Malcolm, a retired computer programmer, was handling business while the "boss" traveled around the four-state area in search of more bargains.

"Malcolm's getting a lot of attention from the ladies lately," Bertie said. "I think he's interested in your mother."

Grace nodded, skeptical. After the nightmare years with her dad, romance hadn't been anywhere on her mom's agenda.

Bertie's pet goat, Mildred, bleated from the goat pen west of the lodge. A houseboat cruised past, sending tiny wavelets against the rocky shoreline below the deck. Bertie chatted a few more minutes, then went back to work.

Grace raised her face to sunlight dappled by a wisp of a cedar branch that overhung the deck. Bertie was right—publicity came with the job. Grace just hadn't been prepared for the sharp sting of bad publicity and untrue innuendos.

Once upon a time she'd been so sure her place was in Branson, making music that would make a difference in her part of the world. But *were* her songs making a difference?

More than anything, she loved to write songs, and to sing and play them. To get paid well for doing something she loved seemed too good to be true. She knew from experience to save for slack times ahead, but even so, she'd been able to help pay off the mortgage on Vintage Treasures.

As blessed as she was, shouldn't she be willing to pay the price with a bad review now and then?

Other local publicity, such as the coverage they'd received on local television stations and in *417 Magazine,* had been top-notch.

The screen door opened again. Grace looked up, expecting to see Bertie or her elderly business partner, Edith. Instead she saw Michael, dressed in black leather. His dark hair stuck out in every direction from the impressions made by his motorcycle helmet.

Warmth curled through Grace's stomach. "Been biking?"

He pulled a chair out and sat across from her. "All the way to Branson and back." His face glowed from the sting of wind, and the fragrance of fresh air hung about him. "Finish your salad and take a walk with me?"

She gave him a narrow-eyed look. "Don't tell me Sherilyn's drafted you into this 'whip Grace into shape' campaign."

"I just thought we needed to have a talk, and it would be more enjoyable if we strolled along the water's edge."

"If it's about the article, I've talked all I'm going to."

"Not that." Michael unzipped his jacket and pulled out some sheet music, which he had secured between jacket and shirt. He slid the sheets across the table for her. "Henry wants us to try this."

The quiet solemnity of his voice alerted her. She read the words and music as she finished her salad. Typical country music fare, with the man complaining because the woman he loved chose to marry someone else.

She looked up at Michael. Still that silent watchfulness in his expression, but why? Over a piece of sheet music? They were always trying new pieces. Granted, she'd been the one to write most of the new songs they'd performed lately, but this was no big deal.

"What's up?" she asked.

"Denton's pressuring Henry to pull some of your songs and replace them with stuff like this."

She felt a stab of disappointment. "Why? He doesn't think business is good enough?" She heard the sarcasm in her own voice, and was ashamed. This job came with its own temptations, and one of the hardest to resist was pride.

He beckoned her with his hand. "You're finished with your salad. Time for that walk."

Michael strolled beside Grace across the broad lawn to the municipal boat dock at the far tip of the peninsula on which the town of Hideaway was situated. She smelled like vanilla and spice and looked like heaven to him, dressed for comfort in old jeans and a hot pink sweater that draped below her hips.

As they walked, he explained his conversation with Henry and caught a glimpse of her eyes as they sparkled with excitement about the television prospect, then darkened with dismay when he explained Henry's concern about the direction of the show. And he told her about Denton's apparent interest in giving Delight more stage time.

She sighed as she stepped onto the unoccupied boat dock and reached into the pocket of her jeans. With a jangle of quarters she purchased fish food from a dispenser, then gave Michael a handful and took some for herself.

"I have to do this every time I come down," she said, effectively changing the subject. Most likely, that had been her intention. She would do almost anything to avoid talking about unpleasant subjects.

Michael tossed his first few pellets into the water. Ducks and geese chattered from the foot of the cliffs across the lake, then began their avid migration as fish gathered below the surface beneath the dock.

He sat down, dangling his legs over the side of the dock, and patted the spot beside him. Grace joined him. By the time they ran out of pellets, the ducks and geese had arrived.

Grace laughed and got up to buy more. "I

also have to do *this* every time I come home."
She returned and gave him another handful
to share with the growing population of hungry mouths.

Michael tossed a single pellet to a solitary
sun perch at the edge of the action. "You still
think of this as home?"

"Of course." She crossed her legs in front
of her to stop the geese from nipping at her
shoes. "As soon as we arrived here from California, I knew this was where we belonged.
I mean, look at this place." She spread her
arms to encompass the broad, neatly trimmed
lawn, dotted with gazebos painted in pastels
of green, pink, blue, yellow and lavender. The
inverted town square, with brick storefronts
facing outward, was encircled by a street on
all four sides. The architecture had a look of
comfort and dependability.

"It's beautiful," he agreed.

"It's a place with roots. The month Mom
and I arrived here, we were invited to the
Hideaway festival, complete with pig races.
Even though I was still injured emotionally
and physically, I couldn't help noticing the
kindness of the people. They welcomed us
with open arms. I met Red and Bertie Meyer

then, and loved them ever after. It broke my heart when Red died."

Michael turned to study her face. "Even though you've only been here since you were sixteen and I grew up here, it seems as if you're as much a native of Hideaway as I am. Do you realize that first Hideaway festival you attended was the first one I ever missed? I was eighteen and off to college. Believe me, if I'd seen you back then, I'd have remembered you."

She laughed, obviously to cover a blush. "You apparently didn't return for several years, because I've never missed one since."

"I worked summers in Columbia to help pay for school, and when I didn't work, I took extra courses. That's why I'm able to do phlebotomy work at the clinic."

"You never came home after you left?" she asked.

"Never enough time," he said. "And with no family here after Dad died, I didn't have a place to stay."

She gave him a look of empathy. As he watched the dazzle of sunlight on her flawless skin, he discovered something he hadn't realized before in five years of friendship. Grace Brennan belonged in the outdoors.

All this time he'd thought she was suited for the stage, with the extravagant lines of her face, her high cheekbones, her finely arched brows, her brilliant smile. But there was something more earthy and natural about her out here in the late-November sunshine.

They ran out of fish food and quarters.

Grace dusted her hands. "How about continuing this walk to the general store? We can get bread to feed these beggars."

Michael laughed and caught her fish-scented hand. "It would be just our luck for Sherilyn to choose that moment to come down and check on you, and she'd have both our hides."

When Grace didn't pull away, Michael continued to hold her hand as they strolled along the grassy shoreline.

"I miss the ocean," she said. "When I was growing up in California, we lived in Thousand Oaks for a while, just a short drive from the beach. I rode my bike there all the time. That's why when those resort people imported sand for a beach this summer, I was all for it."

They reached the sandy beach she was talking about. "I don't know," he said. "I've been to the ocean a few times, and a sandy beach just isn't the same without the ocean waves."

"Better than rocks."

"Have you been back to California since you and your mom relocated here?"

"I went out to visit friends a couple of times, but it isn't the same. Too many memories."

"You've never spoken with your father since you left?"

She shook her head. "He never contacted me after he got out of prison."

"Are you afraid of him?"

Her steps slowed, and Michael slowed with her, still enjoying the feel of her hand in his.

"I'm not afraid of him. I mean, I'm an adult now. What he did he did in a moment of weakness, and he paid for it."

"Have you forgiven him?"

She stopped walking. "He never asked me to."

"Does he have to ask? Forgiveness is for your benefit."

She turned to him. "You've changed in the past couple of years, Michael Gold."

"How's that?"

"You've softened."

He frowned. "Every cowboy hopes to hear those words."

She smiled. "Okay, maybe not softened. You've grown wiser. You listen more. You're calmer."

"Maybe you're the one who's changed." Yet he knew what she said was true. He *had* changed. Some of those changes disturbed him. Some were threatening to take him farther from home.

"You smile a lot more lately," she said.

He squeezed her hand. "I've been spending more time with you, so I have more to smile about."

He knew as soon as he said it that he shouldn't have. She cast a glance toward the road and gently withdrew her hand.

"Okay, what's wrong?"

She shook her head. "I keep expecting to look around and find Jolene Tucker stalking us with her camera and recorder."

"So? It isn't as if we're doing something wrong. People won't be surprised to see a picture of us holding hands."

She looked away.

The disappointment went all the way to his heart. "I get it," he said. "You prefer to be 'just friends.'"

She stepped across the sand. "I don't want to live a romance for the media. I think that would destroy a friendship faster than anything. I'm discovering lately how much I value my privacy."

He followed her. "Let the media create their fiction."

"They don't create fiction, though. They manipulate the truth to titillate readers. I never realized how malicious gossip was until I became the focal point of it."

"You can't ignore the gossip?"

She waved her hand impatiently. "You've been in the public eye long enough to know that what people believe about your life becomes almost as much of a reality as the truth. How many people think you really were driving under the influence, simply because Jolene reported it wrong?"

"I haven't taken a poll." He heard the impatience in his own voice.

"Jolene isn't the only enemy. She wasn't at Friday night's meeting—she only reported what someone else told her. I can't help wondering who's been spying on us."

"Do you see any cast members hanging around watching us?"

As if taking him seriously, she turned and

studied the shoreline, then the dock, then shook her head. "Something else that's been bothering me since Friday—what if Jolene gets wind of the ugly note?"

"What if she does?" he asked. "As I said, you could just come clean. It isn't as if they're going to make a big deal over something you did eight years ago. Do you mind telling me why you're giving Jolene the power to influence whether or not we're able to have a meaningful relationship right now?"

She folded her arms across her chest and studied the shoreline again. "Want to go for a swim?"

She was an expert at changing the subject. "Have you suddenly turned suicidal?"

She laughed. "At least let's go wading."

"Oh, yeah, I remember now. You're the kind who likes to walk barefoot in the rain."

"It isn't a crime. Later we can go canoeing. Come on, Michael, the sun's warm, the sky is clear and we need to take time to enjoy it. I came down here to get away from everything, not argue about work and publicity nightmares."

Without warning, she knelt in the sand, untied her shoes and pulled them off, along with her socks. She rolled up the legs of her jeans, then looked up at him. "Coming?"

"It's practically winter. The water's cold." Grace was nothing if not impulsive.

She shrugged and stepped into the lake, then squealed with laughter at the apparent iciness of the water.

Michael enjoyed the show from his safe spot on the sand. Grace was challenge enough. He didn't need pneumonia to make things more interesting.

Chapter Five

Delight smiled up at the waiter and handed him her menu. "I'd like stuffed mushroom caps and a frozen strawberry daiquiri." If she was going to spend an evening with Denton Mapes, she might as well have some fun with it. She'd try a piña colada next.

"Make that a virgin daiquiri," Denton said as the waiter turned to walk away. At Delight's scowl, the lines of his face deepened with amusement. "Contrary to what you've probably heard about me, I'm not the kind of man who provides alcohol to minors so I can take advantage."

Delight blinked at him. *Whoa, baby, talk about blunt.* "I never thought—"

"I seldom have difficulty finding female

companionship, and I never become desperate enough for it to rob cradles."

She couldn't quite stifle a gasp.

"I have, however, had cradle dwellers attempt to influence me to help them in their careers."

She glared at him. "So you don't rob cradles and I don't rob rockin' chairs. I guess that makes us even."

His eyes narrowed.

She swallowed hard. Now she'd done it. She'd never work in Branson again.

He leaned forward and smiled at her, then laughed.

So the guy was demented. And she wasn't sure she trusted him. Too many men had sworn to her they weren't interested in just her body, then proceeded to prove themselves liars.

Denton gestured toward the western horizon through the plate-glass window. "This place has some of the most beautiful sunsets in the area. That was one reason I wanted to get here early, so you could see it."

If Michael Gold were sitting across from her, the evening would be complete. "So when are you going to get to the point?" she asked. "I mean, we've got the soothin' music, the food's comin', all that." *Watch the accent, Delight.*

He raised an eyebrow at her. "Could you relax for a few minutes and just soak up the ambience?"

She swallowed. *Way to go, Delight-big-mouth. Keep it up and he'll be asking for the check before the appetizer arrives.*

His gaze traveled back out the window to the pink-and-gold sunset. He didn't look angry; in fact, he suddenly looked sad.

Delight took a long swallow of her water. That could mean only one thing. Denton Mapes really was getting ready to fire her, and he felt sorry for her. Of course, if she hadn't made that stupid remark about rocking chairs...

"It's okay," she said at last. "I can take it. I know Henry hates me and wants me off the show. I even heard him practically say so today."

Denton's attention shifted back to her. "You heard that?"

"I was at the theater, and I overheard him talking to Michael."

His gaze chilled. "Henry can't always get what he wants."

Oh, really? "So you're not taking me out to dinner to break some bad news?"

His gaze lingered on her a moment longer than was comfortable. "You really don't know how to relax, do you?"

"If you were me, and the owner of the theater where you worked asked you out to dinner, wouldn't you be a little curious? How'm I supposed to enjoy a beautiful sunset when I'm too busy wonderin' what's going to happen to my career?"

"Take your elbows off the table and lean back in your chair. Sip your drink, pretend to enjoy the sunset and the warmth of the fire in the fireplace. If you can't learn to find some enjoyment in each moment while you're young, by the time you're my age you'll be burned out."

Delight gritted her teeth and did as she was told. Tonight she was finding about as much enjoyment in the sunset as she'd find staying inside the lines of a child's coloring book. And Denton Mapes made her feel like a child.

Grace trailed her fingers in the cold lake water as Michael steered the canoe to the dock, then stepped out to moor it.

The sun had dipped below the horizon,

dropping the temperature at least ten degrees in the past thirty minutes. Her jeans had almost dried where she'd accidentally soaked them in the wading incident, but sand continued to irritate the tender places between her toes.

Michael reached down to help her from the canoe. She stumbled against him. He caught her in his arms, laughing. When she looked up at him, she saw him studying the shore, his gaze flitting in scan mode, a movement she recognized easily.

"Michael Gold, you hypocrite," she said, laughing and drawing away. "You're as paranoid as I am."

"Who, me?" he asked with exaggerated innocence, his focus narrowing to a group of teenagers at a nearby gazebo.

"You're looking for signs of a particular photojournalist—or maybe spying cast members—mingling with the real people."

He grinned. "I know we're not worth a drive to Hideaway, but I can't break the habit of looking over my shoulder. Besides, I know those kids. Blaze Farmer, Justin Cooper, Fawn Morrison—"

"Fine, but if Jolene did just happen to be down here and saw me stumbling from the boat—or worse, wading in the lake this afternoon, with you right there beside me—I can imagine what she'd write about it. She'd be questioning my sanity or my alcohol intake."

"So? Everyone knows you're a little on the weird side."

She made a threatening move toward him.

"Okay, I hate that gossip column as much as you," he said. "But I don't intend to let it run my life, or guide my decisions about things that are important to me."

Uh-oh. *That* thread of conversation again. This time she didn't feel like wading into the frigid water to avoid the subject. "My point is that I can't forget how much it hurt to read that article today," she said. "I know how much worse it would hurt if our friendship were to develop into something deeper—"

"Which I think it already has."

"—and then your name and picture would inevitably turn up with some other woman hanging on to you, and the caption would announce our impending breakup. It's the nature of the media to want to keep things stirred up." She sat down on a concrete bench at the edge of the shoreline. The concrete chilled her. She shivered, wrapping her arms around herself.

He took off his jacket and placed it around her shoulders as he settled beside her. "That's a lame excuse to avoid an important relationship, but at least it means you've considered the possibility."

She looked up at him and got lost in his warm gaze. *What are you really afraid of, Grace?* "I've seen ugly publicity ruin too many celebrity relationships."

"Did you ever think that if they were taking cues from the media, they lacked something to begin with?"

"So what if we did became romantically involved, then decided it wouldn't work?" she asked.

"We know each other better than that."

She drew the jacket more tightly around her and shook her head, staring across the deepening shades of silver on the water's surface, hearing again her mother's words, spoken so long ago, right here on this shoreline. *Grace, it's better to live alone your whole life than to marry the wrong person and suffer for it. Best not to get married at all.*

Best not to get married at all…

Michael sighed, crossing his arms over his chest. "I'm willing to take that risk.

Obviously, other things are more important to you."

She couldn't look at him. *Oh, Lord, why now? Michael's nothing like my father. Why can't I enjoy this relationship? What's wrong with me?*

The trill of his cell phone interrupted the silence. Michael didn't respond.

"You'd better get that," she said.

"It's probably Sherilyn trying to lure me into her web again."

Grace reached into the pocket of the jacket he'd wrapped around her and pulled out the offending device, then checked the screen. It was the theater.

Without thinking she flipped it open. "Yes?"

"Hello?" A slightly familiar voice wafted across the space between them. "I'm sorry, I don't know who I'm calling. I'm with the cleaning service for the Classical Impressions Theater, and—"

"Barb? This is Grace."

"Thank goodness! I saw this number on a pad in Mr. Bennett's office. I just finished calling 911."

"Why? What happened?"

"I think the poor guy's dead."

"What poor guy? Barb, who are you talking about?"

"Mr. Bennett. He was lying on the floor downstairs in the auditorium, white as mashed potatoes, when I came into the theater to clean. I touched him to wake him up, and his skin's cool. Oh, Grace, it's horrible! Can you get Michael Gold? I know he and Mr. Bennett are friends."

Shock washed over Grace. "It's okay. We'll be there."

By the time Delight finished her pumpkin spice bread pudding, Denton had relaxed with three glasses of wine. Maybe he'd get soused enough to give her the keys to his Jag so she could drive it back to Branson.

"Tell me, Delight, why aren't you in college?" he asked. "You seem like an intelligent young lady to me."

"You sound like my parents." Hard as she'd tried to get him to spill his guts this past hour, he'd been disgustingly zipped up, wanting to hear all about her, how she'd gotten into the Branson music scene, and what her plans were for the future.

"Then it sounds as if your parents have some sense."

"I went to College of the Ozarks for a year, but that's such a load. It's a work-study program. I had to work fifteen hours and take fifteen hours of school. Luckily I got a job backstage in the drama department and made friends with a guy who got me an audition for *Star Notes,* and here I am."

"You dropped out of school for a Branson show?"

She grinned. "I promised my parents I'd go back when I was twenty-one if I couldn't make it." At this rate, in a year she'd be back in school. For her, that would be like dying.

Denton picked up his half-empty wineglass and swirled the dark red liquid around as he stared into it. "Education is important. Maybe 'making it' wouldn't be the best thing for you right now." He said the words softly, as if talking to himself.

"Sure it wouldn't," Delight teased.

He looked up at her then. "But maybe you'd be interested in an extra song or two on the show?"

Delight snapped to attention. "You're kidding, right?" *Delight, calm down. Don't go hyper.*

"I'm not kidding. Maybe a duet with Cassidy or Blake."

She nearly squealed out loud. "I'd love it!"

"Come to the theater an hour before practice tomorrow."

Delight gave him her brightest smile. She could have danced on top of the table!

Denton's cell phone chimed, and he pulled it from his pocket. He frowned as he glanced at the caller identification, then flipped open the top. "This is Denton Mapes."

He listened, then his expression turned stony. "When?"

Again he listened. "Who found the body?"

Delight gasped. "Body?"

Denton held up his hand for silence. "I'll be right there." He pressed a button and disconnected.

"Somebody's dead?" Delight asked.

"Our director."

"*Henry?*" Her voice squeaked, drawing the attention of diners at a nearby table.

"Control yourself, Delight. The police are involved. It looks like there's going to be an investigation."

"They think he was murdered!"

Silence descended around them. Denton gave her another irritable glance. "You don't have to blurt the news for the whole world to hear." He pulled out a credit card and motioned for the waiter. "It's time to get you home."

Michael preceded Grace through the emergency entrance of Skaggs Community Hospital and saw Henry's family in the far corner of the waiting room. Henry's sister, Fran, waved Michael and Grace over. Her eyes were red, her nose pinched from crying.

"Oh, Michael, Henry's dead."

The shock hit Michael hard. All the way here he'd prayed that Barb had been wrong, that there had been some mistake. "I'm so sorry, Fran." His voice caught. He reached for Henry's sister and hugged her.

He had known this troubled family almost as long as he'd known Henry. Though Henry and his wife were divorced, she, too, stood in the corner with others in Henry's family group.

"Did they say what happened?" Grace asked.

"It looks like he fell from the catwalk above the auditorium," Fran said. "Or maybe from his office window, though how that could have happened, I have no idea. To get out of his window, he would have had to jump."

"We've had problems with one of the spotlights lately," Michael said. "He might have gone up onto the catwalk to see if he could do something about it."

"But he's so surefooted, and the catwalk has a railing," Fran said. "It's not like he would lose his footing and fall."

"He's been under a lot of stress," Michael said. "Maybe he had a bad spell with his blood pressure and grew dizzy. He might have had a heart attack."

"The policeman who spoke to me explained they have to investigate something like this to be sure," Fran said. "That means there'll be an autopsy, which means no burial until it's complete. That's going to make it harder on everyone."

Fran touched Michael's arm. "Are *you* going to be okay?"

"I'll be fine." He patted her hand and released it. "Will you let me know if you need anything?"

"I will." She hesitated. "You don't…know of anyone who'd want to hurt him, do you?"

Michael hesitated. Some people were still upset about the conference Friday night, but to think someone might have killed Henry over it? Crazy.

"I can't imagine anyone I know doing anything to hurt Henry," he said.

"The woman who found him told me she saw a rip on his shirtsleeve," Fran said. "Like maybe it had snagged on something."

"Did she have any idea what caused the rip?"

"No, it's just one more thing they'll follow up on during the investigation."

Michael spoke with Fran and the rest of the family for a few more moments. His offer to pray with them or call a minister was politely but definitely refused. He said goodbye and walked back outside with Grace.

She surprised him by taking his arm and falling into step close beside him. "You don't look too great. You all right?"

No, he wasn't. "Henry's dead."

"I know." Her voice was soft with compassion.

"Did you ever talk to him about your faith?" he asked.

"Yes, Michael, I did, and I know you did, too. We both pushed for songs that stressed the foundation of our lives."

"Obviously I didn't push hard enough."

"You can't cram your personal faith down someone's throat," she said.

"I could have tried harder. The last time I discussed my faith with Henry, he told me to save it for the songs because he wasn't interested. And so I gave up. Too soon."

She squeezed his arm. "Spoken like a true preacher's kid. Michael, there's no way for you to know about his eternity. It could be that something we said to him years ago finally struck home, and he turned to Jesus in faith in his final moments. We honestly have no way of knowing."

He looked at her in the glow from a nearby security light. "Did you ever consider taking up counseling?"

She released his arm and patted him on the back. "If I did that, I'd have to charge you."

He grinned, but inside the questions churned. If Henry *had* suffered a heart attack, then Michael might have been able to anticipate it if he'd done a brief exam.

Henry, did I let you down?

Chapter Six

Grace pulled into the theater parking lot fifteen minutes before noon on Tuesday—an unusual time to be there during the week. She was not surprised to find the lot filled with news crews, police and curious onlookers.

Interview time.

She had been forced to turn off her cell phone last night, because some creative souls had discovered her new number.

The press would have a field day.

Of course, Grace couldn't miss Jolene Tucker's smoke-blue sedan parked near the back of the building. She would be all over this. No telling what she would try to imply.

"Miss Brennan?"

She looked up and saw a policeman holding the cast entrance door open. He smiled as she stepped into the foyer.

"I'm Detective Abrams, and I'll be your interviewer today." He said the words the way a waiter at a restaurant would say, "I'll be your server today."

Grace returned his smile, hoping he wouldn't notice her watery eyes.

"I've seen your show several times," he said.

She began to relax. Okay, this might not be so bad.

"I know this is difficult," Detective Abrams said, "but we decided it would be easier to gather everybody and process information here at the theater. The auditorium is roped off as a possible crime scene, and we're not allowing anyone inside except those cast members we're questioning." He gestured toward an unoccupied office along the hallway, then closed the door behind them as they entered. "Do you have any thoughts about what Mr. Bennett might have been doing on the catwalk?"

"He could have decided to check out the spotlights. We've had trouble with one of them lately, but it isn't something he typically sees to."

"Who does that?"

"Usually Blake Montana. He's kind of

a jack-of-all-trades, the one we call when there's something wrong with the lights."

The detective pulled a chair out for her in front of the desk, then circled and sat across from her, placing a notebook on the desktop and pulling a voice-activated recorder from his pocket. "Do you mind if I use this?"

"Not at all."

His fifty something face creased with a frown. "Blake Montana? Is that his real name?"

"No. A lot of entertainers use stage names."

"Are the two of you friendly with each other?"

"Sure. Blake's a good musician, and he doesn't have an ego problem."

"How about you and Henry Bennett?"

"Henry was like a cantankerous uncle. We disagreed on a lot of things, but I've worked with him, off and on, almost since I started singing in Branson shows full-time."

"How long would that be?"

"Eight years." Before that she'd worked part-time at every job she could find to support herself through college.

"My chief handed me a copy of an article this morning that described a meeting that took place Friday night," the detective said.

"Henry blasted several people pretty harshly. I believe you were one of them."

Grace leaned back in her chair. This was the worst possible time for Jolene Tucker's observations. "As I said, he could be pretty cantankerous at times."

Detective Abrams jotted several lines of notes. "Did you read Sunday's article in *Across the Country?*" He reached for a manila folder beneath his notebook and started to open it. "I brought the copy with me if you—"

"Oh, please, no." Grace spread her hands out in front of her in self-defense. "I read it yesterday morning. Once was enough."

The detective repositioned the folder beneath his notes. "If the article can be believed, he was rough on you."

"Very."

"And Miss Swenson?"

"Yes, and her."

He looked down at his notebook. "Can you remember if he criticized anyone who wasn't mentioned in the article?"

"No, he didn't." Jolene's spies had been thorough, for once.

"Miss Brennan, I hope you understand I have to ask these questions."

She forced a smile. None of this was his fault. "Please call me Grace."

"Thanks. Grace, would you mind telling me a little about your activities yesterday?"

"I spent Sunday night in Hideaway, slept late the next morning—or tried to, until my agent called and woke me up before the crack of noon. I didn't return to Branson until we received a call from Barb, who works with the cleaning service. She'd discovered Henry's body."

"You say 'we' received a call," Detective Abrams said. "Was someone else with you?"

"Yes, Michael Gold and I were together at the time. After the call we came back to town and went to the hospital."

The detective tapped the tip of his ink pen on the paper and gave her an inquisitive smile. "I understand Gold paid Bennett a visit here at the theater around noon Monday?"

"Yes, but Michael lives in Hideaway, and he came to talk to me after his meeting with Henry."

"So it was a business meeting between you and Mr. Gold?"

He looked disappointed, and Grace suppressed a smile. Even big, tough policemen had a touch of romance in their hearts.

"Michael and I are friends," she said.

"Can you think of anyone who might have wanted to harm Henry Bennett?" Detective Abrams asked.

"Half the cast and crew at one time or another have been angry with him, Detective. But I don't think I work with anyone who would be capable of murder."

He jotted a note. "I noticed the backstage door has a keypad entrance. How many people know the code?"

"Only the people who work here. They change it often."

"Are any doors ever unlocked when the theater is closed to the public?"

"No. Our security personnel are sticklers about things like that."

He leaned forward. "So, if Bennett's death was not from natural causes, it's probable that an access code would have been needed to enter the building and get to him."

She stared at him. "Y-yes. That's…right."

As the detective completed his questions, Grace struggled with the dawning truth. No one got inside the theater on Mondays unless they knew the access number.

It had already become obvious that a cast or staff member was a snitch. Was it truly possible one of her co-workers was also a murderer?

Delight tapped her toe against the leg of her chair as she faced her inquisitor across the table. The guy's military-cut blond hair and blue eyes were the only attractive features in a face that looked like a smile never visited it.

If she had his job, she'd never smile, either. "Is this going to take long?"

"That all depends on the answers I get," he said. "When was the last time you spoke with Henry Bennett?"

She leaned back in her chair and folded her arms over her chest. "Yesterday around noon."

"You practice on Mondays?" The guy stared at her as if he could see the spot on the wall directly behind her head.

"No."

"Miss Swenson, we have a report of a black Dodge Viper being driven from the parking lot of this theater at a high rate of speed, complete with squealing tires, about noon yesterday, and we have evidence to back up that report. Did you and Mr. Bennett have an altercation at this theater yesterday?"

Altercation? Why couldn't he just speak plain English? "Okay, look, it's no secret Henry didn't like me, but Michael Gold was here at the same time, and he walked out with me. I left before he did. Why don't you grill him?"

"Miss Swenson, we have reason to believe you returned to the theater later in the afternoon."

Delight felt a sudden chill slither across her shoulders. "I wasn't aware Denton had hidden security cameras installed." *Careful, Delight. This is serious.*

"Did you or did you not return here a second time yesterday?"

You can't lie, Delight. Tell him the truth. "No use in makin' a big deal of it. I just wanted to return an outfit I'd worn home Friday night. Henry freaks if we take anything home from the dressing room."

The guy didn't look like he believed her, but then, he didn't have much of an expression at all.

He consulted his notes, then flipped the page. She nearly groaned out loud. Judging by his list of questions, they were in for a long session.

* * *

Michael caught sight of a tall, skinny woman with black hair as he climbed from his SUV in the theater parking lot. Jolene Tucker. The woman everyone most wanted to avoid. He'd lost count of the well-intentioned people who had shown him her write-up about his "brush" with the law. At the moment she mingled with a few curious onlookers who were banned from the theater. He hoped she didn't con someone into allowing her inside. The woman was a menace.

Tipping his hat low over his face, Michael pivoted away from the tableau and strode toward the cast entrance. At the edge of his vision Jolene quick-stepped toward him on an intercept course.

He punched in his coded number on the keypad and pulled the door open.

"Michael?" she called as he stepped inside. "May I have a word with you?"

"Sorry, no." He allowed the door to close behind him.

"You can't avoid me forever, Michael." Jolene's deep voice, laced with humor, followed him.

"I can try," he muttered. Yes, his behavior contradicted his upbringing. Dad had taught him to face things head-on, to be polite when spoken to and always to treat ladies with respect. Jolene Tucker, however, had most likely never had that title bestowed on her. And Dad had never taught him how to respond to the venom of vicious gossip.

Moments later Michael sat slumped on a bench in the lobby, elbows on knees as he faced the woman in a navy pantsuit, Detective Rush. She had already asked him the usual questions about the nature of his visit here yesterday, and his whereabouts the rest of the day.

She was a plump woman on the young side of fifty, with graying hair and deep smile lines. "I've heard you and Mr. Bennett were friends. His family speaks highly of you."

Michael swallowed hard. "We met soon after I came to Branson. Are these questions really just routine, Detective?"

She shook her head. "*I'm* supposed to be asking the questions, Mr. Gold," she said gently.

"Michael."

"Thanks, Michael. I'm Trina. Would you be willing to say you've got some hotheads in the cast and crew here?"

He gave her a wry smile. "This is show

business. Egos get bruised easily in our neck of the woods."

"Did Henry Bennett have a habit of bruising egos among the cast and crew of *Star Notes?*"

Michael felt a flash of irritation. "It doesn't feel right to be speaking ill of the dead."

"It wouldn't be right to allow someone to get away with murder just to avoid a few awkward questions."

"So you're saying you really do suspect that this was murder?" he asked. "Is there evidence that suggests it?"

She shifted in her seat, leaning forward. "Right now we're really just covering all the bases. Can you recall the specifics of your conversation with him yesterday?"

"Sure. We were discussing possible program changes requested by the theater owner, Denton Mapes."

She frowned. "Is that typical?"

"No. Henry was the general partner. The boss."

"Were there ever any disagreements between Mr. Bennett and Mr. Mapes?"

"I believe there were." But not enough to incite murder.

"Anything else you can tell me about your meeting Monday?" the detective asked.

"We also discussed the possibility of a television show. Then I asked Henry about his blood pressure, and even threatened to check it myself. He apologized for Friday's outburst and promised to apologize to Grace."

"Was Miss Brennan noticeably upset about his outburst?"

"She's accustomed to his behavior. They've known each other a long time, and she forgives easily."

"But was she upset?" the detective repeated.

"Sure. Who wouldn't be?"

"Did you notice if anyone else was very upset?"

"Delight was stunned, I think. And Mitzi was more flustered than I've ever seen her."

"Mitzi?"

"She's our wardrobe manager. Basically, everyone seemed shocked by the tirade. Do you have any idea when the results of the autopsy will be available?"

She smiled. "You don't give up easily, do you? How about if I call you as soon as I hear something?"

"I'd appreciate that."

"Did Mr. Bennett often work on dark Mondays?"

"Yes."

"So his presence here would have been a matter of general knowledge with the cast and crew?"

"With anyone who knows Henry's habits." Until this morning, Michael had been convinced that Henry's death had been from natural causes, though what he might have been doing on the catwalk had everyone stumped.

"Was he worried about anything in particular?" the detective asked. "Did he happen to mention to you if he was having any problems with anyone at the theater or elsewhere?"

Michael hesitated. "All Henry's relationships had taken a nosedive in the past couple years. He became so driven to produce the best show in Branson, I'm afraid he lost sight of more important things."

She leaned forward, still writing in her notebook. "What would those be?"

"Relationships. The human connection."

She nodded. "Anything else Henry shared with you?"

"Not that I can remember."

The detective watched him for a moment, then closed her notebook and stood. "I'd like to keep this discussion confidential for the time being, if you don't mind. I'd also like to keep it open, in case I have more questions later."

He jotted down his cell and home phone numbers and gave them to her. "Will you be sure to tell me as soon as they have the results of the autopsy?"

"Of course." She shook his hand and left.

Michael sank back onto the bench and leaned against the wall. Could Henry have been murdered? There must be some other explanation.

Delight tapped her toe on the floor, remembering again yesterday's humiliation. "Everybody knew Henry disliked me, but it wasn't as if that was a shock to me. I mean, he's hated me for over a year, and I didn't kill him in all of that time. Why should yesterday have been any different?"

"I don't know, Miss Swenson. You tell me."

"That's what I am telling you. It wasn't. And before Michael says anything about me eavesdropping at closed doors yesterday, I was *not* eavesdropping, even though Henry and Michael both probably thought I was."

The officer's expression lightened, as if

he'd suddenly realized this could become more interesting. Which was exactly what Delight didn't want.

"I just happened to be walking by Henry's door yesterday, and couldn't help overhearing that *Star Notes* might be televised." She spread her hands. "I mean, any idiot would understand how important that is. I stopped in the hallway, and Michael must've heard me, because he opened the door."

There was a flicker of something in the officer's eyes, and Delight glared at him. He looked amused. The first emotion she'd seen in the guy's face, and he was laughing at her.

He closed his notebook. "Miss Swenson, we have your number if we need to speak with you further."

She stared at him. "That's it? You're done with me?"

"For now. You're free to go. Please exit the theater the way you came in. We've got roped-off areas."

He was dismissing her? Just like that? She got up and sauntered casually from the office, relief making her weak.

She'd almost reached the backstage door when voices reached her from the intersecting hallway.

"No changes!" She heard Ladonna's angry hiss. "I can't believe you would even suggest that now, with Henry lying on some autopsy table and the place crawling with policemen!"

Delight stopped. She would have to cross that hallway to get to the door; Ladonna and Denton would see her and probably think she was eavesdropping again. Great.

"As they say, the show must go on," came Denton's voice.

"Oh, stop it with the platitudes," Ladonna snapped. "You think you're going to gain control of the show just because Henry's not around to stop you."

"Henry and I had discussed these changes," Denton said.

Delight turned to creep away before they could see her, but just then Denton and Ladonna reached her corridor.

"Delight," Denton called after her, "what did you want?"

She turned once more. Ladonna brushed past her, fury in every plump line of her body. Her curly dark hair stood out around her head as if electrified.

"I was just leavin'," Delight drawled. "I didn't want to interrupt your friendly conversation."

Denton seemed to relax. "How did your interview go?"

"I wouldn't know what to compare it to. It isn't like I get involved in murder investigations on a regular basis."

He smiled and glanced down the empty corridor. "I'm sure you did fine. We'd better keep our new plans under wraps until all the excitement blows over and things settle back to normal. Give it a week or two."

Delight shrugged and started to walk away.

"One more thing," he said before she could reach the door.

She looked back. He looked more tired than usual, with extra lines around his eyes and his hair not quite in place.

"Did you mention to anyone where we were at the time I received the call about Henry last night?" he asked.

"Nope."

"Don't bring it up unless someone specifically asks you."

"Why not? It wasn't as if we were doin' anything wrong."

"Of course we weren't," he snapped. Then he sighed, closing his eyes. "It just wouldn't be a good idea to stir up any speculation right now," he said more softly.

"Don't worry," Delight assured him. "I'll keep it zipped."

"But if anyone asks, don't lie."

"Okay. Fine. I won't." She reached the door and escaped before anyone else could stop her and ask questions.

Chapter Seven

After two hours of unproductive practice Wednesday afternoon, Grace found herself hating Denton Mapes with a passion, and knew she'd be spending some time in prayer tonight. The man made it obvious Henry's death mattered little to him. He'd insisted the cast come in for practice the moment the police gave the okay. And now he seemed to relish usurping Ladonna's authority in his attempt to move the musicians around in a game of chess, using human beings as board pieces.

Finally Michael, Grace and Blake refused to comply with the changes—which involved a complete restructuring of the song sequences and a gratuitous display of overt affection between Michael and Delight, of all things. Grace battled a twinge of surprising and irrational jealousy. Then, when Michael rebelled, she battled a twinge of satisfaction.

"This is Branson," Michael snapped, "not the Vegas Strip."

Peter gave his drumsticks a final twirl and set them down, then stepped from behind the drums. "Doesn't look like we're getting anywhere today."

Cassidy picked up his cowboy hat from the floor and put it on his head. "Time for home."

"Not yet," Denton snapped. "We're not finished."

"I am," Grace said. "This isn't jelling. We can't change the whole style of a successful show and expect the public to buy it. What we were doing worked."

"Grace is right," Michael said. "Don't fix what ain't broke."

In spite of the tension on the stage, Grace had to suppress a grin at Michael's affected country tone.

"I can't believe you people." Denton clasped his hands behind his back and shook his head as he strolled across the stage. "This show could double its income if we set the stage for that to happen. We need to look to the future, not stagnate in the past." He directed another cool gaze toward Grace. "Don't stand in the way, Miss Brennan. If you want your own agenda, start looking for it elsewhere. This is *my* theater."

Grace held that gaze. "Who said I had an agenda?"

"What is this, Pick on Grace Week?" Michael asked. "First Henry, then Jolene's piece in that magazine, now you."

Peter snickered as he raised his hat from his head and ran his fingers through his sweat-dampened hair. "Better watch out, Mr. Mapes. Look what happened to Henry."

Denton raised a bushy eyebrow at the spiky-haired drummer. "Peter, is that a threat?"

"Course not!"

"Good, because I recently discovered that you spent some time in jail for assault a few years ago."

Shock registered sharply across the boyish features of Peter's face. Rachel, one of the band members, caught her breath audibly from the far edge of the stage.

"Oh, stop it!" Ladonna called from her seat in the shadows of stage left. "How can you all talk like this with Henry lying dead on some cold table? Denton Mapes, you need to pack up *your* agenda and take the rest of the day off. Your contract doesn't give you the right to barge in and take over without consulting the other partners."

"Henry's death gives me that right," Denton said quietly.

"No, it doesn't," Ladonna snapped. "If you want to call a meeting, you call it the right way, and include the show's administrative staff and our investors. Do you want the cast to walk out on you?"

Denton folded his arms over his chest. "I doubt that'll happen," he drawled, as if unperturbed by her outburst. "They need their paychecks. And they still have obligations."

"I have Henry's itinerary from now until the end of the year," Ladonna said. "Until further notice, we need to stick with that."

"Sounds good to me," Michael said. "Ladonna knows this show better than anyone who could be brought in at this late date. If we start changing the program now, we'll lose our momentum. If we end with a healthy crowd instead of a fizzle, we have a chance of jump-starting a good season come March."

The silence hovered for several seconds before Ladonna gestured to the rest of the cast. "You all go on home, and unless you want to see our dirty laundry aired in that trash magazine again, keep this conversation quiet. Got it?"

"Sure, we got it," Cassidy muttered as he strolled across the stage, slinging his guitar over his shoulder as if it were a shovel. "We have to be good little boys and girls while the grown-ups plan our futures for us."

As the others filed out, Grace looked at Delight, who stood in the shadows, uncharacteristically quiet. She was watching Denton, who walked toward her. And for the first time today, he smiled.

What was up between those two?

Michael followed Blake down the steps backstage. Peter trailed after them, nudging Cassidy in the ribs. "Who died and made Denton king?"

"That isn't funny," Blake said over his shoulder as he tied his damp hair back in a ponytail. "Wouldn't hurt to keep your mouth shut every once in a while, Peter. Especially if Denton's going to play dirty with your past."

Peter scowled. "In case you ain't noticed, it looks like he's playing dirty with your girlfriend."

"I don't have a girlfriend."

"Okay, I'll spell it out," Peter said. "Have you seen him with Delight lately? How much do you want to bet—"

"Peter," Blake snapped, "I'm usually a nice guy, but I don't have to be."

"Sorry. All I'm saying is he sure is pushing for more exposure for her. The way he's acting, you'd think he killed Henry so's he could have creative control." Peter glanced over his shoulder toward the stage, as if to make sure Denton wasn't following. "Or who do you think did it?"

"Did what?" Michael allowed an edge to settle into his voice.

Peter made a face at him, apparently unaware of everyone's growing irritation. "Offed the dictator. I mean, it was a stupid move, but the guy was such a jerk lately, I can almost see how someone—"

"Stop it." Michael had never had a hot temper, but the events of the past two days had brought out some unfortunate latent tendencies. He felt his fingers tingle with the urge to clench them into a fist and show Peter the error of his words. "You need to watch yourself more closely, Peter."

He felt a hand on his right arm and turned to see Grace stepping up beside him. She gave him a warning look, and he realized his voice and words had suddenly developed some bite.

"You people are a bunch of grumps lately." Peter shook his head as he rounded a corner toward the dressing rooms.

Grace tugged on Michael's arm and urged him in the opposite direction along the corridor that led to the lobby. He went willingly. He was tired of being here.

Grace said nothing as their footsteps echoed along the quiet corridor. Michael studied the autographed pictures, hanging on the wall, of musicians who had performed in Branson.

"You doing okay?" Grace's voice was gentle, hesitant, as if she thought he might be ready to explode and didn't want to push him over the edge.

"I missed Henry today."

"Me, too."

"Can't figure out why. He was such a curmudgeon lately."

"You're telling me," Grace said with feeling.

"But his moods were directly related to his health. I can't help thinking I should have been able to pick up on any symptoms of illness. I didn't recognize any warning signals that he might have been building for a heart attack or stroke Monday."

"You're saying you'd feel responsible for his death if they discover it was his heart?"

Michael shrugged. "Sounds a little arrogant, doesn't it?"

"Sounds like you think you can play God," Grace murmured.

"Nope, but I should have read the signs."

"You mean like a blood-test result or EKG reading? Come on, Michael, even licensed physicians need to run tests for things like that."

"If I'd been a licensed physician, maybe I'd have known what to look for."

"But if you'd been a licensed physician, you wouldn't have been in Henry's office discussing *Star Notes,* would you? Give yourself a break, okay, superhero?"

He sighed and shook his head. Her pragmatic words had the desired effect.

They emerged into the cavernous lobby with its marble floors and statues of country music legends, which loomed in the dim light like hovering ghosts.

Michael gestured around them. "Sometimes I can't help wondering what we're doing here. What difference are we making?"

She nudged him with her shoulder. "You're the one who's always reminding me that we can't focus on changing the whole world or we'll be overwhelmed. What we need to focus on is being the best at what God created us for. We sing."

"*You* sing," he said. "Sometimes I feel as if I'm just treading water."

She glanced sideways at him with a look of concern. "You can't be serious. The fans love you. I've heard those women cheer when you walk on the stage."

"Cheers aren't something a guy should hang his hat on," he said. "Your passion for what you do shows in every move you make on that stage, every expression on your face, every word you write and sing."

She stopped and turned to him, arms crossed over her chest. Her pink T-shirt was darkened with perspiration from their vigorous practice, and she wore no makeup. Her golden-brown hair fell in tangles around her neck and shoulders.

"You obviously belong onstage," he said. "Sharing that voice, sharing your heart with people who need a message of hope. You're where you need to be."

"You have a message, too, Michael. According to the Bible, when we sing about God, we're prophesying. Musicians have a place of honor in the Scriptures."

He wanted to reach out and touch her face, cup her chin and tell her how much she meant to him. But she already knew. No reason to talk it to death.

He sank onto a padded carved oak bench in the center of the vast lobby. "All your life you had a driving desire to sing. All *my* life I've had a driving desire to heal people. That desire didn't end when I quit med school, and I can't seem to get it out of my mind lately. Being a phlebotomist at the clinic isn't even close to what I once imagined I'd be doing at this point in my life."

"What did you imagine?"

"I wanted to be a medical missionary."

"Deep in some primitive jungle, risking your life, carrying water from a nearby river, operating under extreme conditions?" There was a gently teasing lilt to her voice.

He couldn't miss the affection in that aquamarine gaze. "I've realized recently that I could help a lot of people right here in our own spot in the world. There are so many who fall through the cracks. They can't afford medical insurance, and can't afford not to have it. Our medical system is broken."

"You think you could fix it?"

"Maybe I could be there for some people who need care and can't afford it. We make good money on this show. I'm saving to go back to med school," he confided.

Grace's eyes filled with concern. "You've thought a lot about this, haven't you?"

He nodded. He knew when he did return to school he wouldn't see Grace every day the way he did now. Missing her would be the hardest part, even when she refused to acknowledge a potentially romantic relationship between them.

Med school...could he do it this time? He'd already dropped out once.

They fell silent for a moment, and the grandfather clock chimed from the far corner of the lobby.

"Henry was going to apologize to you for Friday," he said.

"He always got around to that eventually."

"He wanted so much for you. For the whole cast."

There was a long silence. Grace raised her

right hand and dashed at her eyes. "Are you trying to make me cry again?"

"Nope, but he would have wanted you to know."

"I never doubted his dedication," she said. "With Henry gone, we could both be out of the picture here next year, especially if Denton gets his way."

"Denton doesn't understand that you are the focal point of the show."

"That's your biased opinion."

"I've just got a lot of common sense and business savvy," Michael protested. "You write the songs they love the most. You sing those songs with all the emotion that went into writing them. Denton doesn't want a gospel show, but judging by the response we get from fans, the spiritual element is what they come for. They need to be lifted up, reminded that God's there for them through the hard times and will rejoice with them through the good times."

"Wow," she said, gazing up at him with awe. "You know how to encourage a girl."

"I'm only telling it like it is."

"Thank you," she said softly. "Speaking of Denton, is there some kind of connection between him and Delight?"

"You picked up on that, too?"

"She's just a kid, Michael. She's got all these wonderful, high hopes, and she's obviously passionate about succeeding onstage. How far would she go to get what she wants?"

"She's twenty, not twelve," Michael said. "She wouldn't appreciate your interference. Or mine, for that matter." Although he wasn't positive about that. Lately Delight had made it more than obvious that she might not mind his interference at all, in certain situations.

"Grace? Michael?" A female voice echoed through the hallway into the lobby. It sounded like Mitzi. "You two out here anywhere? I thought I heard voices."

"We're here," Grace called. "You wanting to lock up?"

The woman's footsteps echoed in the huge lobby, and she stepped around a bronze statue of a cowboy on a bucking bronco. Her perfectly plucked eyebrows were drawn together in an uncharacteristic look of perplexity, and her short blond hair looked as if it had been freshly washed and left to dry naturally.

"I didn't even know you all would be here today," Mitzi said. "I thought we weren't going to have a show."

"We had rehearsal, though." Michael stood

to offer her his place on the bench. They would have a show tomorrow night—the police had removed all the crime-scene tape. But would the audience stay away from a show with a possible murder hanging over it?

"Mitzi, what's up?" Grace asked. "You look worried about something."

Mitzi glanced over her shoulder toward the corridor. "I need to talk to someone. I think I should call the police, because I forgot to tell them something today."

Chapter Eight

Grace drew Mitzi down beside her. "What is it?"

Mitzi looked down at her hands clasped tightly in her lap. Her eyebrows drew together with worry. "It's crazy. We all know Henry fought with a lot of people these past two years. That's why I didn't even think about this until later."

"Think about what?" Michael crouched beside her.

"Last Wednesday, before everyone came in to practice that new song, remember? I was in the women's dressing room working on Delight's new costume for the roping scene. You know, the one where she's supposed to rope Cassidy and drag him to her?"

"I remember." Grace thought the song was cute, but Delight needed to work on her notes.

"Well, anyway, I heard Henry shouting at someone, and not because they were hard of hearing, you know?" Mitzi's droll voice shot sarcasm through the lobby.

"Who was the other person?" Grace asked.

"I couldn't tell, because Henry was doing most of the talking—or in this case, shouting. I couldn't even tell if the other person was male or female, but it sounded like the voices were coming from the men's dressing room."

"So most likely male," Michael said.

"Not necessarily," Grace said. "It could have been anybody, because the dressing room wasn't in use at that time."

"Or maybe it wasn't the dressing room, but just nearby," Mitzi said. "Anyway, I don't know who it was or what they were doing here."

"Were you able to make out Henry's words?" Grace asked.

"You'd better believe it. He said, 'You think I can't remember faces? It's my job, and I'm good at it. I've got a long memory. A new name and a nose job won't fool me.' Something like that, anyway. He was still shouting when he barreled into the women's dressing room—you know how he does…did, to make sure everything was in order. He saw me there sewing and snapped at me for eavesdropping."

"What else did he say?" Michael asked.

"I didn't give him a chance to say much. He made me mad, and I told him he was a hateful jerk and nobody liked working with him anymore, so if he didn't stop treating us all like second-class citizens, we'd walk out on him one day." Her voice wobbled, and she raised her hand to her chin.

"Wow, Mitzi, you said that?" Grace looked at the wardrobe manager with new respect.

"Yeah, no wonder he threatened to fire me Friday night, huh?" She sniffed and wiped her eyes. "Why did I open my big mouth? Why didn't I just take it?"

"Because he shouldn't have treated you that way," Grace said. "Did anyone come out of the dressing room afterward?"

Mitzi shook her head. "I was so flustered, whoever it was could've walked right past me and left the building while I was yelling at Henry. When I went into the room later, it was empty. I did see Blake up on the catwalk about twenty minutes after that, checking out the spotlight."

"That's nothing new," Grace said.

Mitzi shuddered. "I hate that catwalk. They'd never get me to go up there."

Grace agreed. She was afraid of heights, and she was glad taking care of the spotlight wasn't her job. In this theater, the shadowy passages that led up to the catwalk made her feel as if someone were hiding in the darkness, watching her every move.

"Do you think it was Blake arguing with Henry?" Michael asked.

"I doubt it," Grace said. "He isn't exactly a hothead."

"So Henry could have been arguing with anyone that day," Michael said. "Cassidy, Peter, Blake, one of the other band members or stagehands."

"That's right," Mitzi said. "Should I call the police and tell them what I heard?"

"You could," Michael said. "But what are you going to say? That you heard Henry shouting at someone?"

Mitzi placed her elbows on her knees and rested her chin in her hands with a sigh. "I have to admit there were times when I thought life would be better if Henry just disappeared, but I never wanted anything like this to happen."

"None of us did," Michael said.

Mitzi gave him a strange look. "Seems to me the police still suspect that someone hated him enough to do him in."

"We work with most of these people every day," Grace said. "We know them. You can't tell me we've been working with a murderer all this time."

Mitzi rolled her eyes at Grace. "Honey, you believe what you want. After twenty-four years of marriage, I thought I knew my husband—until he left me for a woman young enough to be his daughter. People can fool you."

"This investigation is just a formality—you wait and see," Grace said. "By the end of the week we'll discover Henry died of natural causes."

"But when I spoke to the detective, he told me to be sure to let him know if I thought of something else that might be important. I think I'll call him in the morning."

Grace nudged Mitzi's arm. "Come on, let's get out of here before we spook ourselves and start jumping at every little sound. I don't like this place at night."

Delight sat in her chair before the long mirror in the dressing room she shared with

Carlotta, Phoebe and Rachel, the three female band members and occasional backup singers in the show. The others had gone home, and except for Cassidy, Blake and Peter, who were loitering in the hallway outside the dressing-room door, the theater was silent.

The guys, however, didn't know how to be silent.

"Cassidy, if you don't watch your attitude with Mapes, you'll find yourself out on your ear," Blake warned.

"Yep," Peter agreed. "You'd better cool it."

"What do you mean *I'd* better cool it?" Cassidy snapped. "Peter's the one who hinted that somebody might want to kill Denton— right to Denton's face."

"I wasn't threatening him," Peter said. "I was trying to lighten the mood. You all take life too seriously. If we don't try to get along with Denton, we'll miss our chance at television."

Delight rolled her eyes at the mirror and put down her hairbrush. Often, after a show, she liked to hang around and soak up the atmosphere, making believe this was her own personal dressing room, and she was the star. The guys were ruining the mood.

"So, Peter," Blake said so quietly that Delight had to strain to hear him, "what about your police record?"

There was a pause. "Nothing much" came the quiet reply. "A guy picked a fight with me at a bar a few years back. I left and tried to drive away. He tried to stop me. I didn't stop."

"You ran him over?" Cassidy exclaimed.

Another pause. "It was dark. How was I supposed to know he'd run out in front of me? The guy ended up in the hospital for a couple of weeks, and I got tossed behind bars."

Delight shivered. She'd heard enough. "Would you guys go home?" she called through the open door. "Practice is over."

They fell silent, but she didn't hear them leave. Of course not. It couldn't be that easy.

She sighed and picked up the sheet music she'd been hoping to memorize tonight. Sweeping out the dressing-room door, she nearly collided with Blake.

"Well, if it isn't the ponytailed wonder blockin' my exit," she drawled. "Blake, your hair's barely long enough to reach that rubber band. Why don't you get it cut?"

"Sorry, Delight." He stepped aside to allow her out. "We didn't know you were in there."

She immediately regretted her words— Blake had a tender heart—but she'd lose face if she tried to retract them. "It's a free country. You can gossip anywhere you want, but it's stupid to do it here."

"You know," Peter said, "for a pretty woman, you sure have an ugly tongue sometimes."

"Can't take honesty, Peter? Now, why don't you three skitter on home and leave me in peace?" She held up the sheet music. "I've got work to do."

"Sure you do," Peter said. "You're just hanging around to see if the self-appointed king of the roost comes calling for you tonight." He chuckled and winked at her. "My sister used to do that in high school, you know? Hang around in the hallway at school to see if the jock of the week would notice her."

"Stop it, Peter." Blake nudged the drummer in the direction of the exit, and Cassidy joined them.

The three clowns had barely reached the water fountain when Blake broke formation and glanced back at Delight. "Why don't you walk out with us? You don't really want to hang around alone here after what happened."

"Oh, give it a rest, Montana," Cassidy said. "Nothing happened here except an old man died of a heart attack doing something he was too old to do, and crashed to the floor."

Blake ignored him, still watching Delight. "Coming?"

She hesitated. This place *could* be spooky after hours. And Blake had that endearing, puppy-dog look in his eyes.

"I could wait around a few minutes," he said. "Those guys can find their cars without my help."

At that moment Mitzi, Grace and Michael rounded a corner at the end of the hallway, heads together, talking softly. They nearly collided with Cassidy and Peter.

Delight grinned at Blake. "Later. You go on. As you can see, the place is crowded. I'll be fine."

He looked almost disappointed as he turned away.

"Um, Blake?" she said softly, then waited for him to turn back around. "Maybe the ponytail doesn't look *that* bad."

He chuckled and winked at her, then caught up with the other guys.

Delight couldn't help smiling as she pivoted and strolled away. In spite of his ponytail, Blake Montana reminded her of her father. Solid. Dependable. Not exactly boring, but predictable. A big-brother figure—the kind of guy who settled down with a good, wholesome woman and had lots of kids and walked around showing people pictures of his family.

She wasn't even close to being in the market for a husband.

She opened the backstage door to find the lights still on. Good. She would get her coat where she'd left it at the edge of the stage, then take her music home and practice on the keyboard until she could get this song right. She'd tape it on the voice-activated recorder. Hearing the glitches helped.

But when she reached the stage, she found Denton sitting at the ledge, legs dangling over the side as he stared out into the empty auditorium. There was something...vulnerable about his expression, about him, like a kid nobody wanted to play with.

He glanced over his shoulder at her. For a moment he just studied her, his expression unchanging.

"Sorry, I didn't mean to disturb you," she said. "I'll just get my coat and get out of here."

He swung his legs around and stood. He picked up the coat, rubbing the back of his hand against the fur. "Do you think I'm trying to be a self-appointed king, too?"

Uh-oh. "You heard the guys?"

"I don't miss much that goes on around here." Instead of handing her the coat, he wrapped it around her shoulders.

She resisted the urge to apologize for the comments he'd heard. That would make it seem as if she felt sorry for him. No man appreciated that.

He squeezed her shoulder and nodded toward the exit. "Since our dinner was interrupted Monday evening, why don't we make another attempt?"

"When?"

"Soon. Perhaps after the Sunday-afternoon show?" This past Sunday had been the final two-show day for the season.

"Sounds good to me."

"We can dine at my place."

She couldn't resist a quick blink of surprise.

He frowned at her. "The curtains will remain open. You can leave if I make one wrong move. Remember, I don't rob cradles, and you don't rob rocking chairs." He switched off the stage lights as they left, then led the way out into the well-lit, unoccupied corridor. He gestured to the sheet music she held in her hand. "Have you memorized that?"

"I'm still working on it, but it's comin'."

He placed his hand at the small of her back. "I'll walk you to your car."

She slowed her steps. "There's already talk about us, and that Jolene Tucker's a bulldog when it comes to makin' up dirt and publishing it for the world to see. Look what she did to Michael and Grace. You're already worried about bad publicity with Henry's death."

He chuckled. "You expect to see Jolene camped out in the bushes with a camera and a notebook?"

"She wouldn't need a notebook, just her imagination or her spy from Friday night."

"In that case, I do have some work I need to finish upstairs in my office. I'll talk to you tomorrow." They reached a T in the hallway, and he turned left while she headed for the exit to her right.

She had almost reached her car when she heard footsteps behind her.

A shot of adrenaline pulsed through her, and she swung around, suddenly ready to scream.

It was Grace, bundled in her long wool coat and matching gray wool cap, face flushed from the cold air.

Delight released a breath she hadn't realized she was holding. "You know, you could warn a person when you're sneaking up on them."

"Sorry. Delight, we need to have some girl talk."

Delight pressed the auto unlock remote button of her Viper. "I know. I'm completely flat on that one song. Phoebe told me, too, and I got a weird look from Blake." She held out the sheet music. "See? I'm practicing tonight. Happy?"

Grace wrapped her coat more tightly around her. "That can wait." She glanced around the quickly emptying lot and stepped closer to Delight. "I want to talk about Denton."

Oh. Delight sidled closer to her car. "Nothing to talk about."

"Honey, you need to tread cautiously. I'm worried about you. I'd hate to see you get hurt."

Delight reached for the door handle. "You sure about that? Maybe you're just afraid he'll give me some exposure on the show." As soon as the spiteful words tumbled from her mouth, she couldn't believe she'd actually said them.

"You should know me better than that by

now," Grace said quietly. "There are people who will try to take advantage of your dreams, Delight. They'll try to take advantage of *you*. Don't let—"

"Hey, you two lunatics!" Michael called from the cast entrance. "Did you realize it's below freezing out here?"

Grace's cell phone chose that moment to chirp, or Delight would've apologized.

Grace shot a glare at Michael's retreating figure, gave Delight a look of frustration, then shrugged and answered her phone. "Hi, Sherilyn. What's up?"

Delight got into her car and drove away, leaving Grace in the middle of the lot talking to her agent.

Grace meant well, but Delight wasn't in the mood for a nursemaid.

This had been a rotten day. Delight had to admit that with Henry gone things really didn't seem to work so well at the theater. And even though she'd resented the man, his death was a tragedy. He'd been a lonely old man who didn't have many friends, just a lot of underlings who were mad at him all the time. He'd died alone at the theater to which he'd devoted so much time.

And even though Delight was thrilled that

a theater owner believed she was star material, most of the cast thought Denton was practically a nut case.

And Grace thinks I'm a silly floozy willing to do anything to get ahead.

Am I?

Was Denton really planning to take advantage of her? A guy could talk a pretty good line when he wanted to fool a girl. But was that what Denton wanted?

Grace stepped into the crowded entrance of Ruby Tuesday's and spotted her agent immediately. Sherilyn's ebony face glowed with a smile that radiated across the room as she waved from a table at the far right corner of the room.

"I thought you'd never get here," Sherilyn said as Grace joined her. "I've ordered for you—hope you don't mind."

"I do."

"Tough. Your water's on its way. Come to the salad bar with me. This is where I want you eating for the next few weeks, if you eat out at all."

"Since when did you become my social director?" Grace grumbled.

"Since I put you on that diet Monday."

"I've got a banquet planned at the Chateau in a little over two weeks, and I'm not canceling."

"Fine, then learn some willpower before the banquet." Sherilyn's dark brown eyes softened, and she reached over and patted Grace's hand. "It's for your own good, babe. You've got some great things in store in your future, and I'll tell you all about one of them as soon as we get our salads."

Grace followed her agent through the crowd and selected the veggies and dressing she was told to take—with no croutons.

Grace asked a quiet blessing over their food before Sherilyn could launch into her spiel.

"You're going to love me for this." Sherilyn's eyes danced with excitement.

Grace picked up her fork, dipped the ends of the tines into the low-carb dressing, then speared some lettuce. This diet wasn't going to be easy after all. She was starved.

"Hello?" Sherilyn waved her hand over Grace's plate. "Are you listening?"

"Sorry. My stomach's growling so loudly I can barely hear you over the noise."

"What would you say to the offer of a recording contract?"

Grace stopped chewing. She blinked at

Sherilyn and slowly placed her fork on the table. "I'd say show me the contract and tell me who offered."

Sherilyn leaned forward. "Ever heard of Dove?"

Grace nearly choked. "No way."

Sherilyn nodded. "They called me late this afternoon. I tried to get you earlier, but you turn your cell phone off when you're practicing."

"What do they want to record?"

"Your songs, Grace. I sent them a demo of your work. They're talking good promotion. For a first-time recording with them, that's excellent. Set your sights on Nashville, lady!"

Nashville! "Do you have a copy of a contract?"

"No, we still have to work out the details. They need to know if you're interested." Sherilyn smiled. "Are you?"

Grace hesitated. "Who wouldn't be?" And yet...

Sherilyn frowned. "Grace, a few months ago you'd have been dancing in the aisle by now. What's wrong with you?"

Nashville. It wouldn't be forever, unless they sent her on a tour. And it might not mean much. This could be the opportunity she'd been waiting for her whole life, but Sherilyn was right. For some reason she wasn't as ecstatic as she'd have expected to be.

She'd received the threatening note on Friday, Henry had died mysteriously Monday. Everything was in an uproar, her whole life was unsettled and she felt overwhelmed.

"Would you give me some time to think about it?" She picked up her fork again. Right now all she wanted was a filling meal, and then a hot bath before curling up in bed with a good book.

Chapter Nine

Sunday afternoon before the show, Michael Gold sat in Henry's vacated office with the door open, listening to the occasional chatter drift upstairs from backstage. In less than a week Henry had died, an investigation had been launched, an autopsy performed and a decision announced. Death from natural causes. Heart attack.

Detective Trina Rush, Michael's interviewer on Tuesday, had been as good as her word and had informed him of the news. But he'd picked up on something in her voice—a small note of doubt.

"A puncture wound on his upper arm," she said when he asked her about it. "They found no evidence of drugs, and we knew he was a diabetic, so it's possible it was merely an insulin injection site."

"Then what are you worried about?" he asked.

"Outside upper arm? That's a strange place for a diabetic to self-inject. Awkward. Did you ever know of him to have someone else do his injection for him?"

"Never. Not Henry. He was an independent old cuss."

"Well, anyway, the official decision is in— he died of a heart attack."

Michael had thanked her and saved her number. All through the funeral service yesterday he'd thought about what Trina had said. Of course, the medical examiner had to be sure of the cause of death or he wouldn't have released the body.

The funeral had generated a media blitz, which in turn had generated another sellout for the show last night.

Michael rubbed his face wearily, then looked at the clock on the wall—the one set in the replica of the backside of a donkey. Show time in thirty minutes. His brain felt like mush. He'd slept a total of three hours at most last night, and he knew fatigue would be apparent in his voice.

Something still bothered him about all this, and though he knew it could just be wounded pride, he couldn't stop thinking about it. Henry hadn't been that sick Monday when they'd been arguing, had he? He'd been even grumpier than usual, and yes, Michael had threatened to take his vitals, but decided not to.

Definitely wounded pride. Silent heart attacks happened all the time. In med school he'd heard horror stories about missed diagnoses. The human body was unpredictable.

The sound of rushed footsteps echoed up the stairwell outside the office door. "Michael, you here?"

Grace. "I'm here."

She rushed around the corner and through the door wearing a buckskin split skirt and vest, with fringed suede boots. Her hair, styled and sprayed for serious hold, curved around her face in spiky tendrils. She'd already applied her makeup for the show and carried the inevitable water bottle in her hand.

Her expression reminded him of a stormy day after a tornado warning. She carried some folded-up pages of newsprint beneath her left arm.

"What's wrong?"

She slapped the pages onto the desk and set her water bottle down. The bottle toppled onto its side, spattering droplets across the desk.

"This is the worst day ever!" she exclaimed as she snatched the bottle from its side. "I haven't even broken the seal on it yet." She shoved it aside and pointed to the top headline. "'Local Star Victim Of Childhood Abuse.'" Her voice held an unsteady tremor. "It's today's copy of *Across the Country*."

Oh, no. "Have you read it?"

"Of course I've read it! Delight brought it to me a few minutes ago." She sank onto the chair in front of the desk, and he couldn't help noticing she avoided eye contact.

"Delight brought it to you? Just before a show?"

"Ladonna's already given her a good chewing out."Grace continued to study the page on the desk. "I can't understand how Jolene could have gotten this information. It isn't as if I go around talking about my past."

He reached for the top sheet, but before he could touch it, she'd snatched it up again, as if unable to sit still and let him read it for himself.

"Here in the second paragraph it says, 'If you've ever noticed that Grace Brennan walks with a limp when she's tired, pay close attention to her autobiographical song "Daddy, Don't." This interviewer wonders why her hyperreligious mother didn't leave the bully sooner. After some checking, I discovered that Grace's father spent time in prison.'"

Grace slapped the page back onto the desk and glared at Michael. "This is going to devastate Mom! And the rest of the article doesn't get any better. The article implies my mom was part of the abuse."

"Knowing Jolene, I'm not surprised." He reached for the paper to read it for himself.

"*Where* did the information come from?" Grace asked again, this time catching his gaze and holding it firmly.

Michael flinched at the accusation he saw clearly in her eyes. "Grace, what are you saying?"

Her full lips tightened into a firm line. She leaned forward, elbows on the edge of the desk. "I bared my soul to you the night Henry blasted me. I told you that the song was autobiographical, and that my father spent time in prison. I don't think Jolene had time to chase down information about him, and she doesn't know his name."

"I agree." He couldn't believe she was implicating him.

"And I haven't told anyone else." She crossed her arms over her chest and closed her eyes with a sigh. "Nearly everything I told you that night is in the article."

He held his breath and waited. This couldn't be happening. And yet, he had to put himself in her place. How would he feel if he were in her position?

She stood up and stepped across the office to stare out the window that overlooked the theater auditorium. "It's already filling up."

"Grace, tell me what you're thinking."

"I'm thinking this article will for sure hurt Mom." Grace glanced over her shoulder at him, then turned back to the window. "Did you…" She shook her head and sighed heavily. "I can't bring myself to ask."

Michael closed his eyes. The question she *wasn't* asking plunged deep into his heart. "You really, truly think I would talk to Jolene about you?" He found it hard to keep his voice gentle. "You're willing to believe I've suddenly discarded every scrap of integrity within me to bare *your* soul to a woman I don't even like?"

"If I hadn't read and reread those words in that trash column—"

"Maybe you should be more concerned about who might have overheard us talking in your dressing room that night." He heard the resentment tightening his voice. "Maybe you should have asked a few more people a few more questions before you came barging up here to accuse me. Do you also think I was the one who reported the details of the meeting last Friday?"

Grace's shoulders slumped, as if she wished she could curl up into a ball and hide from the world. "No way, Michael."

"Ask Jolene yourself, Grace. You know me better than that."

"I'm afraid to get near her right now," Grace said. "My hands may go for her throat before I can control them."

"Maybe she interviewed your mother," he said.

"No. Mom would never—"

"Neither would I," he snapped. "But you seem willing to believe it of me."

She flinched as if he'd slapped her. "I'm sorry," she whispered, turning once again to stare out at the crowd through the window. "I'm *not* willing to believe it. I'm just doing my best to find out what's going on, Michael, and I'm sorry if I've offended you."

Offended was such a tidy word. He felt more as if she'd sucker punched him in the gut.

"That woman is wicked," Grace said.

For the first time, Michael glanced at the other folded sheet of newsprint and recognized the name of the local paper. Curious, he picked it up and unfolded it.

A large square outlined in black in the middle of the sheet stated, "FROM THIS VALLEY THEY SAY YOU ARE LEAVING, GRACE BRENNAN. WHERE WILL YOU GO FROM HERE?"

"What's this about?" he asked.

Grace's eyes darkened. She shook her head. "At this point I'm almost hoping Sherilyn put it in there for publicity, maybe to put pressure on me about the contr—" She glanced at him briefly, then looked away.

"About the what?"

She checked her watch, then gathered the papers she'd brought with her. "It's almost show time."

"Are you talking contracts with Sherilyn?" He stood up and followed her from the room.

"I don't think I should say anything about it yet."

"Afraid I'll spill my guts again?" He couldn't keep the sarcasm from his voice.

She preceded him down the stairs. "I'm sorry," she said quietly over her shoulder. "I should have known better, okay?"

Actually, no. It wasn't okay. He was still smarting from her accusation, but before he could say more, they encountered the rest of the cast on their way to the stage. The show was about to begin and, ready or not, the stars had work to do.

The moment Grace stepped onto the stage she felt the effects of the tension between her and Michael. They moved awkwardly as they interacted, and their voices didn't blend as smoothly as usual. Their smiles to each other lacked the typical teasing warmth and playfulness. It was so subtle she doubted the audience would pick up on it, but she did. Big-time.

Worse, either she was imagining things, or their mood was contagious, because at one point during a number she turned to find Delight with her head down, frowning. Delight usually saved her brooding for offstage.

Why couldn't music be fun again?

And what about that snide little ad in the

paper? Surely Sherilyn wouldn't do that. But someone had. Could it possibly be the same person who had sent her the music box? But how could that person know about the contract offer?

Halfway through the show, while singing backup for a sixteen-year-old girl with braces on her teeth and dynamite stage presence, Grace caught sight of the black hair and angular face of her photojournalist nemesis sitting at the far right end of the third row, camera in hand.

Why did Jolene find *Star Notes* so fascinating lately?

The song ended to wild applause, and the talented teenager skipped off the stage with a smile that revealed every bend of wire in her braces.

After a final glance in Jolene's direction, Grace decided to save her angst for after the show. Tonight she would be willing to talk to the reporter, and she would have some questions of her own.

Michael stared at the golden highlights of Grace's hair as he and the others followed her to the lobby for a casual meet-and-greet with tonight's audience.

Maybe Grace had been right. Maybe the added strain of maintaining a romantic relationship on this show was too much. She wasn't the only one who had become ultra-sensitive lately. Particularly when the press was involved, Michael's hackles rose automatically.

And now Jolene had damaged his relationship with Grace. And Grace had allowed it. And *he* was allowing it.

As they entered the cavernous lobby, Grace turned suddenly and raised an eyebrow at him, then nodded toward a familiar figure at the far end, near the gift-shop entrance. The wicked witch of Branson, with pen and camera instead of the traditional broomstick.

"I'm going to ask her a few questions," she said, and separated from the rest of the cast.

Michael grabbed her hand before she could get away. "Wait a few minutes, okay? Then I'll go with you."

Grace tried to tug herself free. "No, you'll beat her up, and that won't look good in front of witnesses."

He held firm. "I have never hit a woman." Yet. "Talk to the crowd first. They're waiting to meet you."

Grace gave Jolene a final glare, then strolled

toward the press of people with an obviously forced smile. Michael knew she would soon relax and begin to enjoy herself.

Three minutes later, with Michael and Grace surrounded by a crush of fans, a man dressed in cowboy garb parted the crowd and presented Grace with an ornately carved wooden music box. Before she could open it, he launched into a stylized rendition of "Red River Valley."

Michael shook his head. Only in Branson. At least the guy had waited until after the show was over.

When the cowboy finished his song and parted the throng of applauding onlookers, Michael recalled the notice in the Branson paper Grace had brought to Henry's office. *From this valley they say you are leaving.* A line from the song. And the notice in the paper… River…

Could it be a coincidence that this was also a song about a river? He caught Grace's attention and frowned. She shrugged and continued chatting with the fans. Maybe she hadn't yet made the connection. At the edge of the crowd stood Jolene, engaged in an apparently fascinating conversation with her hand.

Michael couldn't help wondering what

would appear in next week's column. Unable to restrain himself any longer, he left the reception line and approached Jolene.

She clicked off her voice-activated recorder and looked up at him expectantly. "Well, hello, Mr. Gold. I thought you weren't speaking to me." She had a deceptively mild voice, and she looked almost friendly.

"I only wanted to ask you one question." He decided not to warn her that Grace would be joining them in a few minutes, and she would most likely have more than one question. "What have we done to offend you?"

The angular lines of Jolene's face creased in growing amusement and surprise. "Absolutely nothing. You're the hottest thing going right now."

"So you want to cool us down a few degrees?"

Her dark eyebrows formed a V across her forehead. "Don't you know anything about publicity, Mr. Gold?" She gestured toward the crowd that continued to linger around the cast, particularly Grace and Delight. "Does this look like my column is hurting anyone's reputation?"

"Who's to say what the crowd would have been without your poisonous input?"

She pursed her lips and gave a disapproving shake of her head. "Why, Michael Gold, I thought Christians were supposed to turn the other cheek."

"Since when did you decide I was a Christian? Was that after your insinuation that I was pulled over for drunk driving?"

"I only reported what I saw as I drove by. Would you like to comment on the cowboy's song? What's this about Grace leaving? And what's with the recent river theme?"

"Who's your inside source here at the theater, Jolene? How did you know to be here tonight of all nights?"

The reporter lowered her dark, mascara-coated eyelashes.

"I see. You're obviously a person of high integrity." He made sure sarcasm dripped from every word. "I knew you didn't have time to do the research you implied you did on Grace's father."

"I'd be willing to bet you a couple of season tickets to Silver Dollar City that business will soar for the rest of the season after today's column."

"So you're trying to tell me that you're attacking us in that trash magazine to boost *our* ratings?"

"Hey, *Across the Country* magazine is *not* a trash magazine." Jolene's suddenly shrill voice carried across the lobby. "It informs country fans about the intimate details of their favorite entertainers. It performs a service."

Michael glanced toward Grace, to see her looking in their direction. She did not appear happy, especially when Jolene excused herself and escaped out the side door.

Grace glared at Michael across the lobby as she made her way toward him. He'd apparently had a change of heart about talking to Jolene.

Michael met Grace halfway. "As I expected, she's not willing to give up anything about her informant."

Grace studied his expression carefully, hating the prickle of distrust generated in her gut. Never in the years she'd known him had she found any reason to doubt Michael's word.

She forced herself to shrug and turn back to the cast, who meandered toward the corridor that led to the dressing rooms. "Hey, everybody, don't forget our Christmas dinner two weeks from today," she called to them. "I have a lake-view room reserved at the Chateau, so you don't want to miss it."

Two years ago, when the show first began, Grace had taken cast members to lunch from time to time to get to know them. Last year for Christmas she'd had them all over to her place after the final show of the season. This year she'd decided to have an event catered at Chateau on the Lake.

She glanced up at Michael, who walked silently beside her. "What did Jolene have to say?"

The moment he looked at her, she realized he'd picked up on the suspicion in her voice. She couldn't help it.

A muscle flexed in his square jawline, and disappointment shadowed his eyes. "Just that she's proud of her work."

Grace couldn't miss the brooding gaze of those dark eyes. "Let me guess—she thinks she's doing us a favor."

He nodded.

She swallowed her frustration. Since when had Michael become a man of so few words? "Please tell me she didn't catch the significance of the song that cowboy sang a while ago."

"So you *did* pick up on that?" he asked.

"And don't tell me you suspect me of that, as well."

She winced at the sarcasm. "Okay, you can back off now. I apologized, and I'm truly sorry I even gave a thought to the possibility that—"

"How about a late lunch?" There was no gentleness in his tone. "We need to have a talk."

"Make that an early dinner and you're on. I have a call from my mom on my cell phone, and I want to see what's up. Want to meet someplace in an hour?"

"How about the new Thai place on 76?" he suggested. "I could use something hot to match my temper right now."

Chapter Ten

Grace checked her watch as she strolled out into the parking lot, glad to escape the stuffy theater but also relieved to see that other cast members and theater staff continued to linger in the parking lot. She had become far too jumpy lately, even during daylight hours.

Though clouds hovered so low they obscured the distant hills, the air smelled fresh and was stippled with snow that drifted gently to the ground, then immediately melted.

The weather had curbed activity in the entertainment section of town. Grace knew the grocery stores would be packed with people buying winter supplies and extra food, in spite of the fact that Branson seldom experienced a major snowstorm. Certainly none had been in the forecast for the next few days.

Welcoming the feel of the cool air on her skin, she dialed her mother's number on her cell phone and strolled around the perimeter of the parking lot. Having grown up in Southern California, she loved to play in the snow—something she'd done as a child only on the rare occasion her parents had taken her to the mountains.

Her mother answered on the second ring, her soft alto voice sounding unusually quiet, even hesitant. "Hi, Grace."

"Mom, I'm so sorry. I don't know how Jolene got that information for her article, but it sure wasn't from me."

"Of course it wasn't, honey." Still the subdued voice. Kathryn Brennan barely sounded like herself.

"I know it must have been a shock for you to read that."

"I worked through all those accusations years ago. I believed I was doing the right thing, and what's past is past."

Grace frowned. "You don't sound right. Are you sure you're okay?"

"I'm fine. Believe me, that article is the least of my worries right now."

"Okay," Grace said slowly. Her mother tended to blurt out whatever was on her mind the moment she thought it. This must be serious. "What's wrong?"

There was an indrawn breath at the other end of the line. "I should come into town. We need to have a—"

"Mom, you're scaring me. Just tell me what it is." Grace turned away from the activity along the street toward a picnic area near the entrance to the theater.

"Henry Bennett's death made the news, too, you know," her mom said. "I read about it myself in *Across the Country* today—and about the investigation."

"We were finally told Henry died of natural causes."

"Other people read that magazine, from all over the United States." This time the pause was longer. "Apparently your father read it," she said at last. "He contacted me today."

For a moment Grace wondered if she'd heard correctly. "After all these years? Just like that?"

"He left a message on my recorder while I was at church this morning."

Grace slumped onto the bench, and she grew aware of a vague ache in her left hip, where her father had injured her fourteen years ago. "I'm not sure what to say."

"Neither was I," her mom said. "He wanted to contact you."

"Why would he be reading that magazine? He always hated reading and he hated country music." Grace did not want to deal with this right now.

"He's been keeping up with news of you for quite some time." There was a soft sigh over the line. "He says he's changed."

"Did you…return his call?"

"Yes."

Grace caught her breath. "And?"

"He does sound different."

"A person can sound any way he wants to over the telephone, sixteen hundred miles away. How did he even find out where we were?"

"He did a computer search for my social security number after leaving prison."

"But that was seven years ago."

A long pause, and then another heavy sigh. "Yes. It was."

Grace's hand tightened on the phone. "Okay, what aren't you telling me?"

"I never thought it would come to this."

Grace waited.

"He called once before," her mom said at last. "He said he wanted to make amends,

send me money for back child support, re-
imburse me for your hospital bills, apologize
to you."

"When did he call you before?"

"After he got out of prison."

Grace's hand tightened on the cell phone
as she struggled with the implications of her
mother's words. "He called seven years ago
and you didn't tell me?" She couldn't prevent
the tone of rebuke.

"Again, I'm sorry." There was a catch in
her mom's voice. "I didn't want to bring back
all the nightmares for you. Or for me, either. I
felt sorry for him. I still do. But you've been
my top priority, and your career was just taking off at the time he called. You didn't need
this complication with him then any more
than you do now."

Grace felt an overwhelming confusion. Her
mother had been trying to protect her, and
she appreciated it. Really, she did. She hadn't
wanted to be in contact with her father; she'd
wanted him completely out of her life.

So why did she suddenly feel disoriented?
All this time she'd thought her father had
been as glad to get rid of her as she had been
to get away from him. What would her reac-

tion have been seven years ago if she'd known he wanted to make amends?

"Grace?"

"Yeah, I'm here." What about forgiveness? She had known for several years that she needed to forgive her father for what he'd done. All this time she'd put it off, making excuses to herself so she wouldn't have to deal with that heavy chore. Had he really changed?

"Tell me what you're thinking," Mom said.

"I understand," Grace said at last. And she did. "If I'd had a child who had been nearly killed by her father, I'd have done the same."

"As I look back on it, I believe I should have told you when he called. You were mature enough to handle it. But you know what they say about hindsight."

Grace raised her free hand and caught a snowflake in it, wishing the complications in her life could melt as quickly as the snow did on her palm. "What did you tell him today?"

"That you were doing well, and that you'd have to decide for yourself whether to contact him or not. I told him not to call you, that you'd call him."

Grace sighed and slumped back on the bench, suddenly feeling the cold. "Thanks for telling him that."

"Do you want his number?"

Not now. She couldn't deal with any more right now. "Save it for me?"

"Of course. Grace, are you going to be all right?"

"Sure I am." She tried unsuccessfully to force some cheer into her voice.

"Can you handle some more interesting news?"

Not today. "How interesting?"

"I've decided to put a shop in downtown Branson. Expand the business."

"I've been telling you to do that for years."

"And I'm coming to your show Friday night with a friend."

"What's so interesting about that? You've seen it at least ten times."

"This friend is male."

Grace straightened. "You're kidding."

"Have I ever kidded about that?"

"Who?"

"Malcolm." Mom's assistant in the shop.

Grace allowed that revelation to sink in. She remembered how, as a small child, she'd been taken on an escalator ride in a department store for the first time. She'd suddenly felt as if the world was moving too fast, and she'd cried to get off. She felt that way now.

"I'll get you some free passes," she offered when she could find her voice.

"Nope, Malcolm's already bought the tickets and made reservations for dinner."

Oh, boy. Mom on a date. "That's wonderful. It's about time."

"I thought so, too."

"Malcolm's really nice," Grace said.

"I know."

"He's cute, too."

"Grace, at our age, 'cute' isn't the term."

"Sorry. Mom?"

"Yes?"

"How did you feel about talking to Dad after all this time?"

"I'm not sure. For so long I've told myself it was the best thing for you never to have contact with him again, but I couldn't help wondering about him, about how he was doing. He's married again, you know."

"He is?"

"He's involved in a Christian prison ministry, working with men who are where he was fourteen years ago."

The day was filled with shocks and surprises. "He is?"

"That's what he said. He also has a five-year-old daughter."

Okay, that was about all Grace could take for one day. She had a little sister. Wow.

"Maybe you both need closure," Mom said.

"You could be right, but I need to think about it."

"Or maybe what you need isn't closure, but a new beginning."

"I thought you said I'd have to make that decision myself." Grace heard the sharpness in her tone again.

"Okay, honey. I understand. I'll see you Friday night."

"Make that Thursday night. I think I'll drive to Hideaway after the show on Thursday. I have an appointment to see Cheyenne Friday morning."

"Time for your yearly physical?"

"No, just a little raspy throat the past couple of weeks. It hasn't affected my singing." Yet. "How about breakfast Friday morning at Bertie's?"

"I'll see you there."

Delight's high heels pock-pock-pocked across the gleaming parquet entryway of Denton's extravagant home. "You didn't tell me you lived in a mansion." This place came complete with Arkansas-stone-and-cedar exterior. A crystal chandelier hung from a ceiling at least fifteen feet high.

"This old thing?" There was a grin of satisfaction in his voice. "It only has six thousand square feet of living space. No one I know would call that a mansion."

She touched the carved oak banister of a broad winding staircase. "Who decorated for you? This place looks like a lodge down at Big Cedar." A fancy hunting lodge, with cathedral ceilings, stuffed animals—real ones—and a painting of old downtown Branson on the wall. It had character.

"I did it myself," Denton said. "I've always enjoyed working with my hands." He gestured toward a wall of windows that overlooked Branson from a tree-lined ridge southwest of the town. "It'll start getting dark in about an hour, and you'll see the lights flickering on. It isn't Vegas, but the lights can be spectacular if you love Branson."

Dark in an hour. When he'd asked her here, she'd pictured them eating with the windows open to broad daylight. "And you do?" she asked as he led her to a plush swivel rocker facing the view. "Love Branson, I mean."

"I grew up here. It's home. There's a spirit

about this place that sticks with a person no matter where he is."

"You like that hillbilly mind-set?" Delight asked dryly. "Like those old cars parked on concrete blocks out in the driveways, junky front yards, workers who don't show up on time, if they even show up at all?"

"Don't blame that on the natives. That's just lazy human nature, and you'll see it all over the world."

She suppressed the urge to roll her eyes.

"Branson's always called me back." He turned a switch on the wall and the lighting dimmed. He stepped to a wet bar. "What would you like to drink?"

"I don't guess you'd make me that strawberry daiquiri you wouldn't let me have last week." *Stupid, Delight. You need to keep your wits about you tonight for sure.*

He smiled and reached into the refrigerator below the bar.

She watched him measure ice into a blender. "You're really going to let me drink tonight?"

"You had a daiquiri Monday."

"It didn't have any alcohol in it," she muttered.

"I haven't changed my mind since Monday."

She scowled, then returned her attention to the view. "It really is pretty up here."

"I used to hunt on this ridge as a kid," he said. "Have you ever tasted fried squirrel?"

She wrinkled her nose. "Not knowingly. Don't tell me it tastes like chicken."

"No, it tastes like squirrel. You've lived a sheltered life, obviously. You've probably never tasted mountain oysters, either."

"You tryin' to ruin my appetite so you don't have to feed me?"

He chuckled. "The food's already prepared, and I don't want it to go to waste."

"Just tell me it isn't something gross."

"I was going to barbecue some roadkill, but I'm glad I didn't, because the sauce could have done damage to that beautiful dress."

She made a gagging noise, then leaned back, fingering the silk sleeve of the dress he had admired. Today she'd chosen her most demure outfit.

The blender whirred. What was she doing here? Never before had she dated a man as old—and as legendary in certain matters—as Denton. She glanced at him over her shoulder. Women apparently found him attractive, but she couldn't see it. And she couldn't figure out why he spent time with her. What would a man with so much experience want with a twenty-year-old girl?

Not that she was an inexperienced girl, of course.

Okay, so she wasn't experienced in *that* way. Her parents still had enough of a hold over her that she'd endured the ridicule from her friends in high school down in Alabama for maintaining her virginity. She hadn't yet met a man who was worth that special prize, and Denton sure wasn't. But would she be willing to exchange that prize for a chance to be a star?

By the time Michael parked next to Grace's car, an hour had passed, and his temper had cooled. To utilize the time while he waited, he'd dropped by Henry's sister's house with some CDs Henry had lent him, then visited an old med school classmate who worked at Skaggs Community Hospital. After that he'd followed up on a suspicion, and called the singing telegram company, then the newspaper office. But he hadn't been able to get the information he'd been looking for.

He walked into the warm restaurant and inhaled the spicy scents wafting from the kitchen. Grace already sat at a booth, and he remembered, too late, that she was on a diet. Fine help he was giving her.

She smiled up at him as he approached, and for a bare half moment a rush of love startled him, in spite of his anger at her earlier, in spite of the damage her words had done to their relationship.

Why did things have to be so hard? Couldn't he and Grace just enjoy their time together, ignore the press and wait until all the excitement about them shifted directions?

But her sudden lack of trust...her suspicion...really bothered him. What had changed? Would she have suspected him under other circumstances?

He felt her attention on him as he slid into the seat across from her. Those aquamarine eyes looked suddenly wide and vulnerable, as if she had a lot on her mind.

"Everything okay with your mom?" he asked.

Grace trailed her right forefinger along the condensation of her water glass. "Remember what I told you about my father?"

"Are we going to start this argument again?"

A frown darkened her eyes.

"Sorry," he said. Best not to begin the evening discussing today's fiasco. He'd get to that later.

She took a long draw of her water and set the glass back down. "Mom's fine. She's expanding her business into downtown Branson, and she's seeing someone. As in dating."

"I thought you said she'd never date again."

Grace shrugged. "People change." She paused and studied the wood grain of the table, then shook her head, as if puzzled. "I mean, they *really* change."

"Well, it's nice to know this problem with distrust doesn't run in the family." He said the words before thinking about the possible consequences. When she winced, he considered having his tongue bronzed. Permanently.

She leaned forward, elbows on the table. "You're really mad about this afternoon, aren't you?"

He spread his hands. "I don't know what to say."

"Say you'll forget about my temper tantrum?"

"I'm trying, believe me, but I can't lie about it." Before he could say more, a waiter came to the table for their order.

Sudden tears glistened in Grace's eyes. "I'm sorry," she said to the waiter. "I'm not ready yet. Would you give me more time?"

Chapter Eleven

Denton set the glass of frozen daiquiri mix, topped with whipped cream and a cherry, on the end table beside Delight's chair, then seated himself across from her. "Our meal should only be a few more minutes. It's in the oven."

She rolled her maraschino cherry in the whipped cream, then plopped it into her mouth and bit into the delicious center. Wonderful.

When she had first moved out on her own, she'd bought a whole jar of maraschino cherries and eaten them all in one sitting. She'd done the same thing with a box of chocolates Blake had given her recently. Of course, if she kept that up, she'd be fighting her weight like Grace.

Grace.

When Delight first joined the show, she'd felt like a freshman in high school, surrounded by a bunch of seniors. Grace had taken her out to lunch and treated her like a friend.

And I was a jerk to her the other night. Could Grace have a good reason to warn her about Denton?

"You prepared dinner yourself?" Delight licked whipped cream from the side of the glass and savored its rich sweetness.

"I told you I like to work with my hands." He took a sip of his white wine—obviously he didn't have the same rules for himself that he had for her. But he seemed to enjoy watching her savor her drink. At any rate, he remained focused on her. As if she was the meal and he had an appetite.

"We're having fish?" she ventured.

"Garlic catfish with roasted peppers, eggplant and good old fried okra, a regular hillbilly delicacy." He affected an Ozark twang that sounded authentic. "Tell me, Delight, when did you learn how to dance like you do?"

Delight couldn't suppress a smile. He liked her dancing? "My girlfriend taught me in sixth grade. That was when I discovered I had a knack for it. But I couldn't do it at home, of course, because my parents thought it was sinful. I took lessons in high school without telling my parents."

"Sinful?"

"We belonged to a strict mission church down in Alabama. If the school had a dance, the church had a party so the kids could have fun without getting into trouble."

"And did you?"

"Get into trouble?" She grinned at the memories. "Sure I did. I'd skip out of the party halfway through and hitch a ride to the dance with my friends."

"Are you a churchgoer now?" he asked.

She considered the question. "Not anymore. You?"

Denton swirled the wine in his glass and stared into it as if it held some mystical secret to life. "Not me. I'm too far gone for God to have anything to do with me."

"My daddy tells me God takes whoever's willing."

"Were you ever willing?"

She suppressed a grimace. Why did he have to turn the tables on her? "Maybe once upon a time, but life's too short to be bossed around when you don't have to be."

"How do your parents feel about that?" he asked, still studying his glass.

"Well, you know, I'm old enough to live my own life, but for their sake I fake it when I'm around them."

He glanced at her then, as if disturbed by this personal revelation. "You don't think that's a little hypocritical?"

"What's your problem?" she asked. "You have some preacher blood running through your veins?" And why was he so worried about it, anyway? She'd bet her car that he hadn't invited her here to show her the error of her ways.

"No preacher blood," he said. "But I've lived a few more years than you, and I wouldn't advise anyone to have the experiences I've had. Too many regrets aren't fun."

She scowled. Just because she didn't live like her parents didn't mean she'd end up a lonely, boozing carouser like him.

"You know what?" she said. "I'm *not* a kid, and I stay away from church because I don't like sermons."

"Then I'll stop preaching."

She glanced over her shoulder toward a formal dining room at the far end of the wall of windows. "You really used to live and work in Las Vegas?" she asked, trying to mask the rumble of her stomach.

"For several years."

A telephone rang in a nearby room, and he glanced at the grandfather clock that kept watch over the fireplace. "I'm sorry for the interruption, but I need to take this call." He got up and strolled through a set of French doors into an expansive office at the far left of the great room.

Through the glass of the French doors Delight saw him pick up a cordless telephone and settle into an executive chair behind a huge, polished oak desk.

She got up and wandered around the room, picking up figurines and replacing them, studying the art on the walls, glancing out the windows. By the time they finished dinner it would be completely dark outside. And then what? How far could she really trust Denton?

Grace glanced down at her menu, feeling overwhelmed. She suddenly didn't want to be here. Why had she agreed to this dinner? And why had she accused Michael of betrayal? He didn't deserve that.

Michael looked up from his menu. "How hungry are you?"

Grace spread her hands. "Not very."

"Trust me to order for you?"

"Of *course* I trust you." She tried to catch his gaze.

Without looking at her, he motioned for the waiter and ordered.

"I really do trust you," she said when the waiter walked away.

Michael nodded, but she glimpsed the doubt that lingered in his expression.

She couldn't blame him. "Michael, I—"

"How much weight have you lost so far?"

"Six pounds." She gave him a tentative grin. "My clothes are already more comfortable, but don't tell Sherilyn I said that. She'd just gloat."

"Believe it or not, I haven't broken a confidence yet."

She felt the barb, and disappointment overwhelmed her. "Michael, I don't know how to convince you how sorry I am."

He held up a hand. "I don't want another apology. I've already forgiven you." He frowned. "I think."

"You *think?*"

"Just because you've forgiven someone

doesn't mean you've automatically stopped feeling the sting."

"Then what do you want from me?"

"I'm afraid I want something you can't give right now," he said quietly, resting his elbows on the table. "You could apologize for the next hour, but today proved you don't trust me. Not deep down."

"I was upset, and I struck out blindly."

"You don't suspect someone you trust of betraying you."

"I didn't realize it hurt you so much," she said.

He spread his hands on the tabletop. "I didn't either. I guess the more I think about it, the more it upsets me." He leaned forward, lowering his voice. "I'm disappointed because I love you, Grace." He stopped and glanced away, as if his own words had startled him.

They certainly startled Grace. They also made her realize how very important their relationship was to her—how important it had been for a long time.

"What really disturbs me is that you've known me for five years," he continued. "If you haven't learned to trust me in all that time, I don't think it's going to happen."

"Michael, I—"

He held up his hand again. "I know this—" he gestured from himself to her and back again "—isn't what I'd thought it could be. Maybe you were right. Maybe this isn't the kind of atmosphere where a healthy romance can flourish."

She felt the echo of his words all through her body. He had been deeply hurt, and she'd been the one to hurt him.

Delight's stomach rumbled again as she strolled through the huge kitchen and inhaled the delicious aromas. Denton obviously made big bucks. This kitchen was four times the size of the one in her condo. He apparently liked to cook.

She set her empty glass on the counter and continued her exploration to the curved staircase. Except for the occasional touches of pure country Ozark, like the primitive wooden rocker on the deck, this place screamed elegance.

Her shoes sank into Berber carpet as she climbed the stairs. She was halfway to the top when lights came on in the upper hallway. Must be motion sensors somewhere. The trill of birdsong drifted through the hallway, followed by the muted strum of a harp. Major motion sensors.

The upper landing also overlooked Branson, and by now a few pinpoints of light dotted the rolling hills. The tower at Shepherd of the Hills glowed with Christmas brilliance. Delight loved Branson during the holidays.

Restless, and getting hungrier by the minute, Delight was about to return downstairs and force the issue when she noticed one closed door. The others stood open, with everything pristine and in place.

Something about a closed door had always piqued Delight's curiosity. Amid the sounds of birdcalls mingled with a flowing brook, she gripped the door's handle and pushed it open.

She flipped the lighted switch beside the door, and a golden glow illuminated a spacious bedroom suite and sitting area, a king-size mahogany sleigh bed with dresser and chest to match. A mural of Ozark forest graced the far wall. She stepped across the room to see if it was an actual painting or one of those wallpaper kits, but before she drew close enough, she spotted a desk in an alcove several feet from the bed...and a framed photographic collage at the corner of that desk.

It was a collage of startlingly familiar photographs—all were of her.

She crept closer as the hairs tingled at the back of her neck. None were publicity pictures. In fact, she didn't even recognize a couple of the photos—they were from a distance…as if the photographer had snapped the shots without her knowledge.

In the central picture she wore an open, friendly smile. Her hair tumbled over her shoulders in a long, tangled mess, and she wore no makeup. She hadn't gone out in public without makeup since her eighteenth birthday.

What was Denton Mapes doing with all these pictures of her in his bedroom?

She heard a soft brush of movement behind her. "Delight?"

She froze.

"Wouldn't you like something warm to drink?" Michael asked, his tone suddenly polite, as if he was already distancing himself from the conversation. "It's cold outside."

She shook her head, took another long swallow of water and put the glass back down. "I've been so thirsty lately. Hot drinks just make me thirstier." The aromas that usually caused her mouth to water now made her feel slight nausea.

"I called the newspaper about that strange ad in the paper today," he said. "Someone paid for it with cash, and they didn't leave a name. Same with the singing telegram. Anonymous. I think it's a pretty good guess that both were connected to the music box you received with the nasty note."

She blinked at him. "You've already checked that out?"

"Of course. I know a few people I can call late on a Sunday afternoon."

She was deeply touched. In spite of his anger, he was still watching out for her. She'd been so scattered after her mom's news that she hadn't even thought to make those calls herself.

The waiter brought the soup. Grace stared at the food, her eyes clouding with tears. Reaction was setting in. She needed to get away, needed time to think.

It was all too much. Any other time she would have told Michael about her discussion with her mother today, asked his advice about the mystery gift giver. Who else could she talk to? Not her mom, who already worried to much. Not Sherilyn. Michael would understand, and he might even drop some tid-bit of wisdom softened with a dose of humor.

But other than his attempts at detective work, Michael seemed to be withdrawing just as Grace was about to open up. How could she have done this to him?

Michael picked up his plate and scooted from the booth. "Come on, let's get some salad."

"I'm really not very hungry."

He stopped and looked down at her, then slid back into his seat. He reached out as if to touch her arm, but drew back. "Are you okay?"

With the tears came the runny nose, and she fumbled through her purse for some tissues. "I'll be fine. It's just been a bad day, that's all. First I read Jolene's outrageous article, then I blow up and accuse one of my dearest friends unfairly and then find out I'm being stalked by some anonymous gift giver." *And finally I discovered that my long-lost father wants to get in touch with me.*

"Do you mean that?" Michael asked, his voice suddenly gentle. "That I'm one of your dearest friends?"

"That's nothing new." She reached for her purse and slid from the booth. "I'm sorry—

if I stay here I'm just going to make a spec-
tacle of myself and embarrass us both." She
was in for a good crying jag. Time to admit
defeat. "Can we take a rain check? I'll treat
next time."

"No, Grace, wait." He reached for her.

She drew away as the tears threatened to
spill from her eyes. Before she could humil-
iate herself and make it harder for both of
them, she walked out the door and into the
snowy night.

"What're you doin' with pictures of me in
your bedroom?" Delight heard the tremor in
her own voice.

Denton looked irritable. "I didn't expect
you to come searching through my bedroom."

"I wasn't searchin'. I was killin' time while
you talked on the phone *forever*—and you
didn't answer my question."

"Aren't you being a little immature? Is it
so unusual for a man to have photographs of
an attractive woman on his desk?"

"In his bedroom?" she exclaimed. "Those
pictures were taken before I even started with
Star Notes. In fact, I don't even remember
some of them. Where'd you get them?"

He watched her in heavy silence for a moment, then sighed. "Would you believe they were sent to me by someone who knew of my interest in you?"

"You *knew* me?"

"Yes."

"I didn't know you." This was creepy. "You're not some kind of stalker or something, are you?"

"Of course not," he snapped.

She flung up her hands. "This is too weird." Grace was right about him.

Delight couldn't go through with a seduction scene tonight or any night with this man—and that had to be what this whole private dinner was about. Maybe her parents had more influence on her than she'd thought. If her friends knew what a prude she still was...

But no way would she sell her body for a show, not even for star billing, which Denton had never promised her anyway.

Of course, he'd never touched her, never made a move....

For a moment she tensed. She had to go past him to get out of this room. Would he grab her and not let her leave? He was accustomed to getting his way with women....

She looked up to find him watching her

with rapt attention, as if he'd been studying the expression on her face.

He held a hand out to her. "Delight, there's something I haven't told you."

She stepped away from him. "I think I know all I need to." Suddenly she wanted to be as far away from the man as she could get. What had she been thinking? Had she stooped so low, gotten so desperate for success, that she'd consider selling her body like a prostitute?

She pulled her cell phone from her purse and walked from his bedroom. "I'll call myself a cab."

Chapter Twelve

On Friday morning Grace gave in to the delicious guilt of Bertie Meyer's black walnut waffles as she sat across from her mother at a table that overlooked the lake at Hideaway. Maple syrup pooled in the crisp squares, mingling with melted butter in a heady aroma that could make a person high.

Her mom pushed her empty plate aside and leaned forward. "Have you called your father yet?"

"Nope." Grace refused to be rushed into something she wasn't emotionally prepared to do. She placed another succulent bite of the waffle into her mouth.

"Not that I'm nagging," Mom said.

Grace smiled at her and continued to eat. At forty-nine, Kathryn Brennan was a knockout, with a quick smile that radiated warmth and kindness, and gamine features that made her look ten years younger. People often mistook her for Grace's older sister.

Kathryn never sat still for long; she talked with her hands, and she had a charming quality about her that made people want to do whatever she asked.

There were times, like now, when Grace would even call her a steamroller.

"Looking forward to the date with Malcolm?" Grace avoided her mom's pointed stare, turning her gaze to a flock of Canada geese taking a sabbatical in Table Rock Lake.

"Very much." Kathryn yielded to the unspoken request, and proceeded to fill Grace in on some particulars of the date plans and her hopes for expansion of the business.

Grace finished her waffle and scraped the plate with her fork. She wouldn't have a chance like this again for weeks, and she wanted to savor every bite.

"Is your throat still acting up?" Mom asked.

"A little." *A lot.*

"Very bad?"

"Nothing to worry about, I'm sure. It's probably just stress." *Either that or I'm never going to sing again.*

"What time is your appointment?"

Grace checked her watch. "In about fifteen minutes."

"Does this thing with your father have you that upset? You've lost weight. I'm worried about you."

Grace shook her head. "I've lost weight because Sherilyn has me on a strict low-carb diet so I'll be in shape for a television promo shot we're doing during a Christmas show. The weight loss is a good thing." Why was it that mothers were the only ones who didn't see their daughters' physical flaws?

"So you're not worried about talking to your father?"

"I'll be fine with it. Honest. I just haven't worked up the nerve to call yet, okay?"

"Then you're not fine with it."

Grace sighed. Kathryn Brennan was relentless.

"You know, honey, you're right about too much stress. It's more than any sane woman should have to deal with."

"I'm in show business. Sanity has nothing to do with it."

Mom frowned at Grace's lame joke.

"Sorry." Grace decided not to mention the contract Sherilyn had been nagging her about this past week. "Don't worry about me so much. I'm a grown woman, and I'll be okay."

"What about those anonymous gifts you've been getting? And that strange ad in the paper Sunday? Everyone's talking about them."

Grace refused to give in to the temptation to spill her guts at this point. She'd begun to brace herself for another little surprise after every show. No more had arrived yet.

"Sometimes that goes with the job," she said at last. It wouldn't do to let her mother know how tense she'd been lately, how frightened she'd become about going home alone in the dark. Even driving down from Branson last night, she'd glanced in her rearview mirror a few too many times.

"Do you think someone connected with *Star Notes* might be doing a lot of this stuff to boost sales?" Mom asked.

"Could be." Grace wanted desperately to think that was the extent of it. Information was definitely being leaked from an inside source.

Grace knew the police could probably track down more about the music boxes and the ad, but she didn't want to go to the police. No crime had been committed, and they would likely tell her there was nothing to investigate. But she was spooked by all the things that had happened lately.

"Anyway," she continued, "I've worked with a lot of the cast from time to time over the years. Many of them are new, like Delight, Peter and Cassidy, but Ladonna, Blake, Rachel and Phoebe have been in Branson as long as I have. I know these people. I can't imagine any of them betraying their co-workers."

The years seemed to have enhanced a certain quality of fire in Kathryn Brennan's blue-green eyes when she felt passionately about something, as she seemed to at the moment. "I think you should be a little more cautious, Grace, especially with Henry dying so recently. Someone thought his death wasn't an accident, or the police wouldn't have been so quick to investigate."

"I'll be careful," Grace assured her. "But the medical examiner has ruled that Henry's death was from natural causes."

"Even medical examiners have been wrong, you know. At least we can trust Michael. He would never do that to you for any reason."

"No." Grace checked her watch again. "I'd better head toward the clinic so I won't be late."

"You've got ten minutes, and it's just up the

street. What's with you and Michael lately? Every time I bring up his name, you change the subject. Is there other trouble brewing with *Star Notes?*"

"You mean other than the fact that Henry is dead, the remaining leadership is at loggerheads and Denton is threatening to delete several of my songs from the repertoire?"

"Other than that," her mom said dryly.

"That about covers it." Grace sighed and thought once more of Michael. She felt as if an invisible hand had reached into her body and was squeezing the life from her heart.

She grabbed the check, hugged her mother and practically fled to the clinic.

Michael unlocked the front door of Hideaway Clinic and flipped on the lights as he entered, glad no patients had arrived early.

Ordinarily he didn't work at the clinic on Fridays, but Dr. Cheyenne Gideon had expanded hours and opened two more exam rooms last week. Demand had expanded along with the clinic.

Both Cheyenne and Karah Lee Fletcher, the other doc who worked here, kept busy with an ever-increasing load of patients as

Cheyenne continued her quest to have the clinic designated as a rural hospital.

Michael was just turning on the lights in the clinic proper when the front door opened. He peered through the reception window to find Grace stepping inside, looking delectable in khaki slacks and a ribbed turtleneck the color of hickory nuts.

He hid his surprise with a casual wave. *Relax, Michael. You know she wouldn't be here just to see you.*

"Hey. What's up?" he asked.

"My weight after breakfast this morning." She frowned at him. "I thought you only worked here on Saturdays."

He grinned. "They got lucky this week. As Cheyenne always says, business is booming."

Grace strolled over to the coffee table in the waiting room and picked up a magazine, then settled onto the sofa, clearly prepared to wait.

He allowed his gaze to linger on her a moment longer. She'd obviously lost weight, and she looked good. But Grace always looked good to him. Every single day.

They'd been stilted with each other since Sunday, and Grace didn't let the dust build up under her feet when the show ended at night.

"You're not sick, are you?" he asked.

Grace shook her head, glancing up at him. "You remember I mentioned the other day I was having trouble with thirst? Something's bothering my throat, as well."

"Sore? Need a strep test?"

"No, it isn't sore, but it's been tightening up recently. Cheyenne's helped me a couple of times in the past."

"Probably stress."

"I can't imagine why," Grace said dryly as she tossed the unread magazine back onto the coffee table. She glanced back at him, then down at the floor, then stood and strolled across the room toward him. "Michael, I—"

The back door burst open at the end of the long hallway behind him, and Gavin Farmer—aka Blaze—came barreling into the clinic, tugging off his heavy overcoat.

"Hi, sorry I'm late. I overslept. Dane's gone soft on me, and he doesn't make me get up and milk anymore since I've practically started living here." Blaze had beads of ice threaded through his kinky black hair, attesting to the fact that the teenager had apparently showered just before crossing the lake from the boys' ranch that was his home.

He hung up his coat in the break room, then

joined Michael at the reception desk and spotted Grace. His black eyes widened, and he suddenly seemed to lose his ability to speak. Michael could have sworn a flush deepened Blaze's ebony skin.

"Uh. Hi."

Michael restrained his guffaw with difficulty. He had seldom seen this wonder teen at a loss for words, but everybody in the office knew Blaze had a humongous crush on Grace.

She gave him one of her brightest smiles. "Blaze! I was hoping you'd be here today. Out of school for Christmas break?"

The kid swallowed audibly. "Uh...not yet."

"Well, take time to enjoy it when it comes. Don't let them work you through your whole vacation."

"I heard that." Cheyenne Gideon's voice sounded from the rear entrance. "Stop trying to influence the help, Grace."

Before Blaze could recover his command of the English language, Cheyenne personally escorted Grace to a treatment room and closed the door behind them.

Blaze looked at Michael. "You've known her for five years, and you haven't married her yet? Man, I thought you had a brain. I should grow up and marry her myself."

"You'll have to learn how to talk around her first."

"You talking about Grace?" A voice came from the entry.

Both men looked up to see white-haired Bertie Meyer striding toward them carrying a pink bakery box. She placed it on the counter. "Sarah told me to drop these off for you. Don't let Karah Lee eat any of those doughnuts. She's about to backslide from her diet."

"I'll make sure she doesn't see them." Blaze took the box into the break room.

Bertie glanced around the empty waiting area. "I thought I saw Grace come in here a few minutes ago."

Michael jerked his head toward the exam room. "Cheyenne already took her back."

Bertie gave the waiting area and door another fleeting look, as if to assure herself no one else was within earshot, then rested her arms on the counter and leaned toward Michael. "What put that hangdog expression on your face?"

He smiled into the wise old eyes of the lady who had been like a grandmother to him for more years than he could count. "I don't have a hangdog expression now that you're here."

"Don't start that with me, young man. I saw Grace come in here earlier, and I think the same thing that's eating you is eating her."

Michael resisted the urge to roll his eyes. The nice thing about small towns was the sense of belonging he'd always felt here, even after his family was gone. The bad thing about small towns was the open-door policy. Everyone knew everyone else's business and took a personal interest in it. Too personal.

"Work's not the most fun place to be right now," he said. "We'll get a break soon, and things will smooth out."

"You know, it's a funny thing about problems at work. They don't seem nearly so bad when you share the load with good friends. But when those friends are at cross purposes, the whole world seems darker."

He nodded. "You taken to mind reading in your old age?"

She chuckled, her blue eyes gleaming, and the ageless Hideaway rhythms caught Michael in their allure…that old bond of community. "Nope, just the grapevine alive and well. Whatever it is, you two kids can work it out. I've been waiting a long time to see you set that friendship to a new tune."

"Would you be too disappointed if it didn't happen?"

"Would *you?*"

He would be devastated.

As Bertie gave him a casual goodbye wave and left, he felt some of the heaviness lift. Bertie was right—he and Grace *could* work things out if they would. But would they?

He could give Grace the time she needed to come to grips with their relationship. He loved her enough to wait until she discovered that she truly could trust him. Nothing was ever as dark as it sometimes seemed. God was in control of this romance, after all.

Aren't You, Lord?

More patients arrived for their appointments, and Dr. Karah Lee Fletcher came breezing through the back door, red hair sticking up in all directions. She and Blaze began their usual morning fight over the doughnuts, and Michael realized he truly was a blessed man.

He knew at that moment, with absolute clarity, where he belonged in the scheme of things here in Hideaway. They would need another doctor here someday. It was time to take his future in hand and make things happen.

Grace watched as Cheyenne entered information on the computer in the treatment room. She was a beautiful woman with high cheekbones, olive skin and rich black hair. She had given up a lucrative career in emergency medicine in Columbia, Missouri, to move here and establish this clinic.

"Hoarseness, huh?" Cheyenne unwrapped a tongue depressor and pulled a small flashlight from her pocket. "How long has this been going on?"

"A couple of weeks."

"Since before your director's death?"

"It began around that time, I think."

Cheyenne did a quick check of Grace's vitals, then replaced her stethoscope around her neck. "Your rate's a little fast. Your speaking voice isn't hoarse, but that doesn't necessarily mean anything."

"The hoarseness comes and goes. It isn't as bad this morning as it was last night during the show. If it gets worse, I don't know what I'm going to do."

"Are you taking any medications that could

be drying you out? Antihistamines for a cold, maybe?"

"I know better. I don't even touch caffeine. And I drink practically a gallon of water every afternoon during practice. It's a running joke at the theater that I can't practice if I get too far from my bottle. But my mouth still feels so dry."

"How dry? Like it's filled with cotton?"

"Stuffed to capacity."

"Any sore throat? Burning?"

"Nope."

"No history of reflux disease?"

"None I've noticed."

"And you've only been bothered by the problem when you're doing a show?"

"That's when it seems the worst."

"Have you had any extra stress going on lately besides Henry's death?" Cheyenne arched a dark eyebrow. "Or is that a stupid question?"

Grace grinned at her. "I would never call you stupid."

"Anything I can help with?"

"Stomp some toes at the theater so everyone will stop fighting, find out who's been leaking information to the press and also who's been having music boxes delivered to me during or after the show."

"I did hear you've been under the gun."

"My actions onstage are wooden, I'm feeling more and more paranoid and my voice has cracked a couple of times."

"Dane and I attended the show a couple of nights ago, and I didn't notice a problem."

"No one's mentioned it, but I can hear it myself."

Cheyenne pulled her chair from behind the computer and sat down across from Grace. "I know you don't want me to medicate you for the stress."

"That's right."

"How many hours a day do you use your voice?"

"We practice at least two hours, then perform two."

"And you sing most of the songs?"

"Yes, either as soloist or harmony."

"Are you singing any more than usual?"

Grace frowned. "We seem to be practicing more new pieces, but I wouldn't say there's a whole lot more."

"How do you feel after these sessions?"

"Exhausted."

"Why? You're young and strong. You shouldn't feel so tired after a simple practice."

Grace regarded her physician with curiosity. "You think there's something else going on here?"

"I'll order a blood draw and do some testing, but for now, stress seems to be the causative agent, except for the dry mouth. That doesn't sound like stress." Cheyenne reached for an order sheet on the small treatment-room desk and jotted something on it, then frowned. "I notice you've lost some weight. Bertie says you're on one of those low-carb diets."

Grace nodded. "If you tell me that's causing the trouble, my agent will hire a hit man to shoot you."

Cheyenne smiled. "Tell her to back off. I haven't heard of dry mouth as a side effect of those diets, but they do cause fluid loss, and that could cause dry mouth. I've never liked the idea of quick weight loss."

"I'll be sure not to tell Sherilyn."

"For now, however, we'll keep watch on you. Keep drinking the water." She paused for a brief moment, her dark eyes narrowing. "Do you drink bottled water?"

"Yes. I buy a case at a time."

"In the unlikely event that you've purchased something with a contaminant in it, try switching brands." Cheyenne got up and went to the door, then turned back with a cheesy grin. "Brace yourself. Michael's our phlebotomist this morning. You'd better hope he's in a gentle mood."

Chapter Thirteen

When Delight arrived at the theater Friday evening she noticed that the only other cars in the parking lot belonged to ushers, ticketers and concession-stand workers. And Denton Mapes. He'd driven his Jag.

She'd avoided him since Sunday, ignoring the two messages on her answering machine, making sure she stayed with others in the cast when at the theater.

She entered through the front lobby instead of the cast entrance, greeted Helen and Ben at the ticket counter and hovered at the new gift shop window display. She would avoid the backstage area for a few more minutes, coward that she was.

A teenage girl stepped from the ticket line

and shyly approached Delight. "Aren't you in the show?"

Delight nodded and smiled.

"What's it like to work with Grace Brennan? Is she as nice backstage as she is on?"

Delight swallowed her disappointment, making sure nothing showed in her expression. "She's even better."

An older woman spoke from the line. "So sorry to hear about her abusive childhood."

"I was, too." Delight sweetly excused herself and escaped.

As always, music from past performances drifted down from overhead speakers, with Grace's clear voice singing "Daddy, Don't." Delight heard her own voice harmonizing, along with Michael's and Blake's, until Grace took her solo to the upper ranges of the rafters, a cappella.

Delight stopped walking and listened. Really listened.

For a moment she held her breath, and in that moment she heard the true notes of the song for the first time with honest appreciation. Grace hit every note with perfect pitch, and with such appropriate emphasis that the song had the power to bring tears.

Delight closed her eyes. She'd tried often

to match the heartbreaking vibrato in Grace's voice. Last time she'd listened to a recording of her own voice—this morning, in fact—she'd realized that when she tried to sound like Grace she actually sounded more like a kitten trying to cough up a hair ball.

Grace's voice brought out a deep blend of emotions, from grief to humor to worship, coming from deep within herself...or maybe it came from somewhere outside herself. Maybe Grace really did have a special connection to heaven.

Delight knew her own feet were firmly planted on this earth.

As if held by the power of her discovery, she strolled to the end of the corridor to the group entrance and glanced at her reflection in the plate glass.

More than anything in the world she wanted to see that reflected image at center stage someday. She wanted to walk through the lobby and hear her solo voice raising the rafters, have people step out of the ticket line just to talk about her, not to ask her about someone else.

One day...

Someone appeared in the reflection behind hers. She stiffened.

"You haven't returned my calls." The crackly tired voice of Denton Mapes sounded in her left ear.

She whirled and looked up into his craggy, lined face. Instinctively she stepped backward.

He sighed with obvious weariness. "Would you mind telling me why you're shying away from me like a wild animal all of a sudden?"

She glanced past him. They were alone in the wide corridor.

"Delight, you act as if I'm going to attack you. Would you relax?"

"I can't help it. I was stalked once, when I was sixteen, and that's what this feels like."

"I'm not a stalker. I'm—"

"And the pictures? You had my pictures in your bedroom." She could still close her eyes and remember the tenth-grade dropout who had developed an insane crush on her, carrying her picture around in his billfold, telling people he was going to marry her.

One night, when she'd skipped out of a church party to go riding around with friends, the dropout had followed her into the mall parking lot and grabbed her from behind.

Good thing she had a strong voice.

"I don't think we've got anything to talk

about," she said. "If that means you're going to fire me, then you'll just have to fire me."

"Forget about that," he snapped. "I'm not going to use my authority to force you to listen to me, but I would like to be able to talk to you without feeling like a dirty old man."

Delight blinked at him. That had been pretty much her opinion. Older man hoping to get lucky with a young, reasonably attractive musician and willing to dangle a carrot of career in front of her to lure her in, just as Grace thought.

"I don't know how many times I have to tell you that I am not interested in you in a physical way," he said.

Delight suppressed a snort. "Do you have any idea how many times I've heard that line? 'Oh, Delight, it's not your body I'm after. I love you for your mind.' What a crock."

"You're comparing me to your high school dates?" Amazingly, in spite of everything, he sounded amused. A little irritated, maybe, but amused.

"You want to hear something strange?" Delight asked. "For some crazy reason I can't even understand, something my parents preached to me actually stuck. My body is mine, and it never belonged to anybody else—except God, according to them—and it's not going to belong to *you*. If I don't have the talent it takes to make it in this business, then I'll go back to college like my parents want me to do, and I'll learn some other profession."

"That statement is a testament to your immaturity," he said quietly.

She glared at him.

"Only the arrogant and the very young think that just because they have talent they can take on the world without any formal training or experience." He gestured toward the autographed photos of country stars on the walls of the corridor. "This town is packed with talented musicians. Your father knows that, which is why he's willing to give you a taste of the competition so you'll realize what you're up against."

"If you feel that way, why are you trying so hard to give me more exposure? Why *me?*"

He hesitated, then looked beyond her. She turned to find a bus unloading its tour group directly outside the doors.

Time to leave. "We don't have any more to talk about," she said as she rushed past him.

* * *

Grace entered her dressing room to find Delight sitting in front of the makeup mirror, staring as if mesmerized by her own reflection. When she caught sight of Grace, she flushed.

"Hi," Grace said.

Delight turned on the stool to face her. "I was hoping you'd show up before I had to go get dressed."

Grace laid her purse on the table behind her. "This is a surprise. What's up?"

"Got any advice for someone looking for a job in Branson?"

"Sounds serious. Do you have a friend who's out of work?"

"Nope, but I doubt I'll be asked to renew my contract for this show."

"What makes you think that?"

Delight swiveled away from the mirror and leaned forward, elbows on knees. "I'm not exactly popular around here right now, and there's no way that's going to change." She sighed. "I'd be willing to take any of your leftover offers."

Grace pulled a bench over and sank onto it. "What happened to you and Denton? I thought you were buddies."

"You don't have to rub it in." Delight fingered an eye-shadow container on the makeup table. "I know you warned me."

"I wasn't rubbing anything in. Denton has more contacts in show business than I do. If you're friends—"

"Which we're not."

"What happened there?"

Delight scowled at her. "I told you not to rub it in."

"Did he try something?"

"No, but..." Delight glanced toward the doorway, then lowered her voice. "I'm just staying away from him, okay?"

"Has he done something to make you uncomfortable?"

Delight blinked up at Grace, as if surprised by the concern in her voice. "It looks like he's got a...thing for me. Why else would he be pushing for me to sing the songs *you* should be singing?"

"Maybe because he sees your talent and energy. It never hurts to plan for the future."

Delight shrugged, then allowed her hands to fall gracefully onto her lap. "But you're doing great, the show is successful. I mean, Michael's always saying if it ain't broke, don't fix it. So what's Denton tryin' to fix?"

Whoa. This kind of admission from Delight Swenson? Grace could hardly believe her ears. "He wants something new for the show, and he knows I'm not willing to do everything he wants."

"Obviously neither is anybody else," Delight said. "So why isn't he listening?"

Grace shrugged. She couldn't claim to know the mind of Denton Mapes.

"So you want to tell me what I'm doing wrong?" Delight looked up at Grace, her eyes stormy blue and troubled.

"Who says you're doing anything wrong?"

"Henry, for one. Remember he told us we needed to give each other pointers? You were supposed to teach me how to sing, and I was supposed to show you how to lose weight and dress right. Your weight's going in the right direction." Delight gave Grace's clothing a disapproving look. "But you could still use some help with wardrobe."

"Maybe you can take me shopping someday."

Delight nodded, obviously gratified. "The only other secret I can help you with is cinnamon."

Grace leaned back. "Cinnamon?"

"I eat it all the time. It's supposed to keep

your blood sugar down, which keeps you from getting hungry. And I hear it's good to lower cholesterol, although I'm not worried about that. I soak cinnamon sticks in water until they're tender, then rinse them and eat them. You have to watch for the woody stuff, and don't smile without first checking to see if you've got it between your teeth."

Grace grinned. "That's how you keep your figure?"

"Well, okay, that and I exercise constantly."

"And maybe also because you're twenty."

Delight shrugged. "There are lots of people my age who can barely waddle into the theater. So what's your helpful hint to reach stardom?"

"I've got two of them. One is time."

Delight rolled her eyes like a recalcitrant teenager. "I should've known you'd say that, but what about those hot stars who hit the charts long before they were my age?"

"I can't speak for them, only for myself. It took me a lot of time to gain recognition, and even to convince someone to look at the songs I wrote."

"What's the other hint, besides the fact that I need to work on my voice control?"

"The most important thing for me was to sing for someone besides myself."

Delight raised a hand. "Hold it. I know where this is headed. I'm going to get a sermon."

"I'm just telling you how I feel about my place in the music business," Grace said. "I'm not trying to tell you what to do. For me, it isn't a business. My life wouldn't end if I left Branson tomorrow and never came back. I would always sing for Him, either at church or on the street corner or in the privacy of my own shower."

Delight took a soft breath and let it out slowly, holding Grace's gaze steadily. "You really mean that, don't you?"

Grace nodded.

"I probably ought to apologize."

"For what?"

"I've been kind of a jerk to you lately. I think, down deep, I kind of blamed you for what Henry said to me, and don't even ask me why."

"He was pretty rough, Delight."

"I know. I guess you could say I'm a little competitive."

Grace suppressed a snort of laughter. "A *little?*"

Delight grimaced. "Anyway, I shouldn't

have shown you that article Sunday just before the show. That was tacky."

"I would have seen it sooner or later. Sherilyn would have made sure of it."

"Not just before a show."

"True."

"I'm sorry about the thing with your father," Delight said.

"Thanks. I don't know how Jolene got that information. I certainly hadn't intended it to become public knowledge."

"You probably didn't intend your fight with Michael to become common knowledge, either, but everybody's watching to see what's going to happen next with you two."

Grace grimaced. "They can back off."

"But that's one reason I feel bad about showing you that article. You two had your fight after that."

Grace didn't feel like baring her soul to Delight. "I jumped to a hasty conclusion, and I shouldn't have. I was totally at fault." That was all the explanation Delight would receive.

Delight grinned and had started to speak when a thump echoed from the far side of the room. She cried out and reached for Grace as the door to the wardrobe room opened and

Mitzi came breezing in, carrying several outfits over her arm.

"I had to take up the silver lamé, and the star-spangled blue isn't far behind. You've got three outfits preset in the quick-change room." She stopped when she caught sight of Delight. "There you are. You've got a new outfit change, too. Better get into the other dressing room and check it out. Grace, I brought new earrings for this red dress. Let's see how it looks on you before I do the preset on it."

Delight glanced toward the wardrobe door, then looked back at Grace and raised an eyebrow. "Do you keep that door locked?"

"No way." Mitzi answered for Grace as she spread her burdens out across the dressing bench. "I need access to these rooms, and I don't want to have to carry a ring of keys around all the time."

"Don't you think that's a little risky?" Delight asked. "I mean, considering all that's been going on here lately?"

Mitzi gave her a look of exasperation. "Last I checked, unlocked dressing-room doors don't cause heart attacks. As far as I know, that's the only thing that's happened around here."

Delight gave Grace another pointed look, then shrugged and left the room.

Michael was halfway through the final song before intermission—a love ballad to a couple in their eighties who were celebrating their sixty-fifth anniversary. Grace came down the steps from the stage on cue to join him in the final chorus of "Love for Eternity."

Before she reached his side, she darted a glance toward the far aisle, where two men were coming toward them, wearing tuxedo T-shirts and the familiar black top hats of a local special delivery service.

Between them, they carried an elegantly wrapped package at least four feet long and three feet high. Grace missed a beat as the men advanced toward them between the front row of seats and the stage.

As the music ended and the crowd cheered the faithful couple, the deliverymen reached Grace and Michael.

The crowd continued to cheer as the men placed the package ever so gently in front of Grace. They bowed, handed Grace an embossed envelope, waved to the audience and left.

Michael could see the alarm Grace tried

hard to hide. Holding the envelope as if it might contain a deadly virus, she returned to the stage and gave the usual invitation for the audience to visit the gift shop, take advantage of the concession stand out in the lobby and come up front to meet the cast of the show.

"What's in the package?" a man yelled from the middle of the theater.

Grace gave him a smile. "I'm afraid to find out."

"Open it!" exclaimed an elderly lady in the front row.

Grace glanced toward Michael, who gave an imperceptible shake of his head. Whoever had sent the package had timed the delivery to give the impression to the audience that they were meant to share the moment.

More people from the audience urged Grace to unwrap the package.

With barely concealed reluctance she returned to the mysterious object wrapped in iridescent shades of silver and gold. She tore at the paper until it fell away, and the crowd gasped. So did Grace.

"It's a Lladró!" cried a lady from the front row.

"A collector's piece, for sure," called someone else.

Michael moved down for a better view, and saw an exquisite figurine depicting Cinderella arriving at the ball in her chariot. The title of the figurine was "Cinderella's Arrival."

"This is too much," Grace whispered, showing Michael the card she'd received. It read, "Midnight is coming faster than you think."

As soon as they broke for intermission, Michael raced backstage and took the corridor to the lobby. He ran outside into the parking lot, to find the delivery van pulling out onto the street.

He ran to his dressing room and looked up the number of the delivery company. The person he reached informed him sweetly that their customer wished to remain anonymous, and they were required to respect the wishes of their clients.

He hung up, frustrated, and went to the green room, where stagehands had carried the amazingly elaborate figurine. The whole cast had congregated around it.

"Thing's probably worth thirty thousand or more," Delight said. "I know, because my mom collects Lladró figurines. She'd be drooling all over this thing." She looked up at Grace. "Someone's either crazy about you or they're trying to make some kind of major statement. Publicity stunt, maybe?"

"That's what I'm wondering," Cassidy said from his backward perch on a straight-back chair. "How about it, Grace? You doing this for publicity? People are freaking, for sure."

Grace raised the card that had come with the figurine, and read it out loud. "I wouldn't write myself a note like this."

Cassidy looked skeptical. "I don't know about that. Think of the attention that thing could draw. You going to tell Jolene?"

"No, I'm *not* telling Jolene."

"Tell the police," Michael said softly. "Only the police can convince the delivery service to reveal the identity of the sender. A paper trail would—"

"I won't call the police, either," she said.

"Why not?" Cassidy taunted. "It seems to me if you were really concerned about these so-called threats, you'd be willing to have them checked out."

"We've had far too much publicity about this already," Grace said. "Somebody's already getting a big thrill out of the attention these gifts are receiving."

"Pretty expensive thrill," Delight murmured.

"We need to stop allowing deliveries during the show," Michael said. "I'll talk to Ladonna and Denton about it."

Grace caught his gaze for a moment, and he could see the apprehension clearly in her eyes. Someone was going to a lot of trouble and expense to spook her. Why…and what would they try next?

Chapter Fourteen

The night of Grace's banquet arrived at last, and Grace stared out the window of the private dining room at Chateau on the Lake, enjoying a spectacular view of the water from her seat at the head of the banquet table. As she watched, the waiters raised the shades in an evening ritual that paid homage to the sunset.

Grace knew from experience that the deepening shadows of pink, evening mauve and smoky-blue would caress the remainder of daylight from the sky in a living display straight from the Master Artist.

Because of the ambience of this exclusive restaurant it had always featured among Grace's favorites. The seating for twenty was just the right size.

Tonight she hoped to repair a special bond

with the people with whom she'd spent most of her waking hours for the past two years. Lately there'd been more show of temper and less camaraderie. She hoped the elegant Christmas atmosphere would soothe everyone's feelings.

Sherilyn Krueger breezed into the room behind the restaurant hostess. The agent wore a satin gown the color of port, which set off the ebony glow of her skin.

She hugged Grace, then settled into the plushly upholstered, carved wood chair to Grace's left. "Honey, you look wonderful in anything, but that green is your color, like an Ozark hillside in the summertime."

Grace smiled her thanks. "Thanks. And you look beautiful, Sherilyn, as always."

Her agent sighed. "If that's true, then why don't I have a date? And where's Michael?"

"He's coming."

"But not with you." Sherilyn's full lips turned down in a teasing pout.

Time to change the subject. "Did you see anyone else arriving?"

"Ladonna and Mitzi and their dates just stepped out of a stretch limo, dressed to the nines."

Mitzi, Ladonna and dates made their entrances and allowed the hostess to seat them beside Sherilyn and Grace at the table.

Mitzi introduced everyone, then sank into the chair across from Sherilyn and picked up a cobalt-blue water goblet. "Grace, you've outdone yourself this year." She indicated the ice sculpture centerpiece, complete with poinsettias frozen inside. "Private dining room with a view? Christmas red, green and gold napkins and tablecloth and candles? Classy as always." She leaned forward. "Twenty people must be costing you a fortune."

"Hush, Mitzi," Ladonna said. "It's not polite to pry."

"I'm not prying. I already know what a meal for two costs at this place. A spread like this would be out of my league."

"That all depends on your priorities." Ladonna allowed the hostess to place the dinner napkin over her lap. "With tonight's box office receipts, Grace can afford this."

Grace grinned. Income for the show remained steady in spite of the slower winter season. They no longer had the sellout crowds of a couple of weeks ago, but this year was probably the best Denton's theater had seen in a long time.

"Any news about the television promo next week?" Mitzi asked.

"Still going forward as planned," Ladonna said. "But just because they're taping the show for a promo doesn't mean we're in. Denton doesn't know everything."

"He thinks he does," Mitzi said.

Ordinarily, television might be exciting, but for some reason Grace felt tired. She'd lost focus, and she needed time to retreat from the world and regroup. Time for a trip to Hideaway for a few days, but that would have to wait until after next week, when they had their final Christmas show.

She still didn't know what she was going to tell Sherilyn about the recording contract. This reluctance to commit obviously frustrated the agent, who couldn't understand the hesitation, especially when she'd been working so hard to get Grace into Nashville.

Another subject that weighed on Grace's mind was her father. After she'd walked out on Michael at the restaurant that night two weeks ago, she'd called her mother for her dad's telephone number and had carried it around in her purse ever since. But she hadn't yet called—what on earth would she say to him?

The banquet room gradually filled with cast and crew, dressed in their finest. Michael entered wearing a midnight-blue tux, and Grace caught her breath. Of course, in the show he wore a variety of costumes that set off his dark good looks, but he seldom wore a tux onstage. And Michael Gold's offstage dress was usually motorcycle or cowboy gear.

His gaze scanned the room until he saw her, and he gave a brief nod, those smoldering eyes lingering on her. But he directed the hostess to seat him at the far end of the table.

Grace felt a fresh stab of disappointment, for which she chided herself. Since the painful scene between them at the restaurant two weeks ago, Michael had been watchful and considerate, but he'd kept his distance, for the most part. It felt as if he were attempting to prove to her how little he needed her company.

Or maybe he wanted her to realize how much she needed his.

Their only meaningful conversation, other than those few moments at the clinic, had involved his failed attempts to discover the origin of the extravagant Lladró porcelain figure, and his repeated requests that she call the police.

He was probably right, but Grace cringed to think of the media blitz that another police investigation might attract. Or would the police even take the time to investigate? After all, sending anonymous gifts wasn't a crime.

Following in Michael's wake, Delight made an uncharacteristically subdued entrance with Blake Montana. She looked like a dream in ocean-blue silk, with her hair caught up in a charmingly loose chignon. Blake's light brown hair, freshly cut, gleamed with blond highlights in the subdued lighting. His handsome features showed well with a beautifully cut suit of finest wool.

They settled next to Michael, whom Delight greeted with effusive attention.

Michael stifled a sigh when Delight made herself comfortable in the chair next to his. Since their conversation the day of Henry's death, the girl had become increasingly clingy, particularly the past couple of weeks.

She turned to her date and placed a hand on his arm. "Blake, I guess you know Grace probably won't be supplying any alcohol for this party, and I've been craving a frozen strawberry daiquiri for weeks. Want to get me one from the bar in the Library Lounge?"

Blake scowled at her. "It's illegal to provide alcohol to minors, and if I remember right, you just turned twenty a couple of months ago."

She pouted and ostentatiously batted her eyes at him. "Please? Just one?"

"Promise you'll stop at one?"

"Have you ever seen me drunk?" She grinned up at him with a smile of innocence. "I just want to get away with something, okay? That little ol' thing won't even give me a buzz."

Blake shrugged. Michael shook his head. After all this time, hadn't Delight discovered that Blake was a teetotaler? Michael felt sorry for him. He obviously adored the young woman, who could have passed for a daughter of Heather Locklear. To Delight's credit, she probably didn't realize the depth of Blake's devotion. Most men responded to her appearance and charm with that overeager, puppy-dog expression.

When Blake excused himself from the table, Delight scooted her chair closer to Michael's.

He glanced longingly toward Grace.

"I need to talk to you about somethin',"

Delight said, her Southern drawl more evident than usual.

"Oh? What's that?"

She glanced down the length of the table. Grace, as usual, was surrounded by people who all seemed to be seeking her attention at once.

For a moment she seemed to grow aware of Michael's and Delight's interest. She glanced toward them, and he thought he saw a tender wistfulness in her eyes. For that one moment he couldn't look away.

Then the headwaiter approached Grace, and the moment vanished.

The cinnamon scent of Delight's breath wafted past him as she leaned closer. "How well do you know Mitzi?"

Michael raised his eyebrows. "Why?"

"Well, if you're still trying to figure out who spilled the beans to Jolene about that awful meeting with Henry, Mitzi's got my vote."

"What makes you think that?"

"Don't you think she might've resented Grace just a little for getting her in trouble with Henry? I mean, he *did* threaten to fire her because Grace didn't wear the outfit Mitzi set out for her."

"Everyone knew that was a bluff."

Delight shook her head. "That's not all. Mitzi's always moving around between the wardrobe and the dressing rooms. She could pick up a lot of confidential information. Kind of makes me wonder if she and Jolene might be friends."

Just then Cassidy Ryder entered the room wearing a Western-cut, silver-studded black tuxedo with black cowboy boots and a bolo tie.

"Oh, brother, would you look at that peacock," Delight muttered.

Michael watched Cassidy make his way to the central section of the table. Like Delight, Cassidy had major ambitions, and he was talented. But his was a new name in Branson, and he made it clear to anyone who would listen that he didn't think he should have to pay his dues the way other musicians did.

Unfortunately for him, every move he made and every song he sang telegraphed his high opinion of himself. Michael had attempted to warn him gently about his stage presence. Dumb idea. Cassidy was in for a rude awakening.

Once again Michael glanced toward Grace, to find her watching him.

* * *

The chatter around Grace seemed to blend into one long, pointless monologue as she tried hard not to watch Michael and Delight with their heads together at the far end of the table.

Why had it taken her so long to realize how much Michael's friendship meant to her? She didn't want that friendship to change…and yet it already had.

She'd half expected to see some stupid article by Jolene about their "lovers' quarrel," but the reporter had shifted her attention toward other entertainers the past two weeks, mercifully ignoring the *Star Notes* cast.

Sherilyn leaned close to Grace's left ear. "Did we enter another dimension when we stepped through that door?"

Grace frowned at her.

"I *mean* what's with you and Michael, and why is he cuddled up to Delight down there?"

"He's not cuddled up with—"

"You want me to scoot so he can sit by you?"

"No, I don't want you to scoot." Grace failed to keep the sharpness from her tone. "Michael can sit where he pleases."

Mitzi leaned across the table. "Didn't you

hear, Sherilyn? Grace and Michael are in the middle of a cold war."

Grace resisted a prickle of irritation. "There's no war."

"Well, whatever it is, I wish they'd patch things up," Ladonna said. "It's affecting the whole mood of the show."

"*I'm* not the one affecting the mood of the show," Grace snapped.

"Hey," Mitzi said, "it's party night. We can argue about work later."

Grace took a deep breath and grimaced. "Sorry." What was wrong with her tonight?

"What else is up with *Star Notes?*" Sherilyn asked.

"Same old thing," Ladonna said. "Denton's still pushing for changes. He thinks he knows what's best, and we've pulled out the contract and discovered the wording isn't specific enough to deal with this situation. Who'd have predicted Henry would drop dead of a heart attack?"

"So in other words, you're telling me you don't have a boss right now?" Sherilyn asked.

"We haven't had a partnership meeting yet to vote for a new general partner or a new director," Ladonna said. "Henry was both. Denton obviously wants more control."

"Oh, my goodness, would you look at this," Mitzi hissed.

Peter entered the room wearing a three-piece pin-striped suit, hair neatly combed. A stunning woman with perfectly coiffed blond hair held his arm. She wore a shimmery floor-length gown the color of cedar berries.

Sherilyn gasped. "Where on earth did Peter snag a date like that?"

"I don't believe it," Ladonna said. "I know that woman. That's his mother!"

Mitzi giggled. "His girlfriend broke up with him last week." She glanced at Grace. "Seems to be something in the air."

Grace scowled at her as more guests arrived and filled all but two of the remaining seats at the table. Denton Mapes arrived last, with none other than Jolene Tucker on his arm.

The room fell silent.

Jolene wore a shimmery silver gown that hugged every inch of her painfully slender body. Her black hair framed her long, narrow face in curls that softened her angular features.

Denton and his date took the only seats left, across from Cassidy Ryder. The awkwardness intensified until Jolene glanced around the table and greeted everyone.

"Don't worry, I left my recorder and notebook home tonight," she announced, apparently not the least bit intimidated by the cool reception.

Chatter at the table slowly returned to normal.

The waiters delivered crusty rolls, shaped by hand, in wire baskets, with swan-shaped butter centerpieces in each basket.

Sherilyn gave Grace a warning look and handed the nearest basket to Mitzi. "Keep that out of Grace's reach. She's lost twelve pounds in two weeks, and I want her to lose twelve more. Doesn't she look great?"

"She looks wonderful," Ladonna said, "but she always does. Don't get too carried away with this weight-loss stuff, okay, Grace? After a certain age a woman needs a few extra pounds to keep the wrinkles from becoming too obvious."

"Thanks," Grace said dryly. She glanced toward Michael's end of the table to see Blake handing Delight a glass with a frozen drink, obviously from the Library Lounge, complete with whipped cream and a chocolate-dipped strawberry on top.

Delight was being treated to an alcohol-free frozen strawberry daiquiri, Grace gathered, from the look of her disappointment when she tasted it.

Grace took a sip of her Perrier and focused on not staring at Michael like a lovelorn schoolgirl.

"Hey, Grace!" Peter called down the length of the table, loudly enough to be heard in the main dining room. "What's this I hear about you getting a major recording contract from Nashville?"

Chapter Fifteen

The chatter subsided, and Michael turned his full attention to Grace, feeling guilty that he found himself enjoying her discomfiture. In spite of her protestations of trust, she had proven that she didn't trust him after all, when she'd been unwilling to confide in him about the contract two weeks ago.

"Does that mean you're leaving the show?" Delight asked. "Can I have your dressing room?"

Mitzi and Ladonna glared at her.

Delight held her hands out to her sides. "It was a joke. You people don't have any sense of humor. I think it's about time some of your writing hit the big time, Grace."

Grace shot Delight a warm grin. "I haven't

signed any contracts, and no, you can't have my dressing room."

Sherilyn held up a hand. "Yet. She hasn't signed yet, but there's a good one waiting for her if she'll make up her mind."

Grace gave her agent a pointed glare.

Sherilyn shrugged. "Best to get it all out in the open. And there's no way you'd have to quit the show. Not unless your concert tour interfered with the schedule at the theater."

"Concert tour," Cassidy muttered quietly so that his voice didn't carry to the far end of the table. "Why the big secret in the first place?"

"Because it's nobody's business," Delight said. "I sure wouldn't tell you bozos about any offers I had. You might blab it to the wrong person, just the way—" She broke off and glanced at Jolene, then looked down at her plate.

Michael could almost feel the mob mentality take over at the table as Jolene became the focus of attention. Why had Denton brought that troublemaking reporter here?

Jolene's laughter lilted down the table. "Any Branson musician would love that kind of 'blabbing.' Admit it, Ladonna, you've sold more tickets in the past few weeks than you sold in the past two years, and this isn't even high season."

"I don't think we're willing to pay that high a price to sell more tickets," Ladonna snapped. "I'd just like to know your source."

"Sorry." Jolene retained her expression of casual amusement. "That's classified. All the publicity's just kicking up the numbers in Grace's fan club, like I've been trying to tell you people all along, but you won't listen to me."

"*Our* fan club," Grace corrected. "They come to see and hear all of us, not just me."

"Yeah, sure," Peter said. "Quit the show and see how many encores we'll be doing. Are you sure you aren't leaking that stuff to Jolene yourself, just to boost the ratings?"

His mother gently nudged his arm.

Michael couldn't help admiring Grace's composure as the razzing continued. He caught her gaze, and she smiled and shook her head.

"I'd like a few of Grace's breaks," Rachel murmured.

"She manufactures her own breaks," Cassidy said.

"If she made this break, why hasn't she already taken it?" Blake asked.

"If Grace isn't interested in a contract, I wish she'd steer it my way," Delight told Phoebe softly across the table.

Phoebe rolled her eyes. "They're talking about a recording contract, silly, not a contract to see how many body parts you can expose without getting arrested."

Rachel giggled, Delight blushed and Michael tried not to smile. The rest of the guests turned their attention to the meal as the first of the appetizers arrived.

In spite of all the explanations, Michael continued to feel a frisson of disappointment at Grace's unwillingness to confide in him.

A cell phone chirped, and Grace watched as Jolene pulled a titanium phone from her clutch purse and excused herself from the table.

Mitzi leaned toward Grace. "What do you want to bet she rang herself so she could escape the table and call in an exclusive report?"

"Calm down." Ladonna leaned forward and lowered her voice, glancing at Denton. "I'd never admit this to Jolene, of course, but ticket sales don't lie. She's right about the increased publicity. And you know how much I hate to admit she's right about anything."

Another cell phone shot its signal through the room, and Grace thought of her dad. She should call him.

Even more important, she needed to forgive him.

She knew what it meant to be in need of forgiveness. She needed Michael to forgive her. How could she expect something from him that she herself couldn't give?

How would she feel if Michael *never* forgave her?

She watched Michael as he carried on polite conversation with Delight and Blake, then laughed at something Rachel said.

Grace thought about her father again. The more she thought about it, the more she was becoming convinced that her relationship phobias had nothing to do with publicity, and everything to do with her father.

As the waiters took dessert orders, Grace tried to give herself over to the sheer beauty of the sky as it turned deepest purple against the silhouette of tree-lined hills in the distance. But her mind continued to return to her father.

All the emotions she'd kept stuffed inside

for fourteen years threatened to overwhelm her. In her heart, she'd been afraid that might happen if she opened herself to romantic love. After all, the only close relationship she'd had with a man had ended in destruction.

She remembered tender moments with her dad, like the days he'd picked her up after school and taken her to ride the ponies at a local park, or when he'd accompanied her and three other giggling seven-year-olds to the beach.

Unfortunately, other memories eclipsed the good ones, like the one-way screaming matches behind closed doors, the sound of slapping and her mom's cries of pain.

As a well-known chef and part owner of one of the most exclusive restaurants in Ventura, California, Tyrel Babcock had given his family a good life once upon a time. They'd lived in a gated community on a hillside overlooking the ocean. But then his partner had embezzled funds and they lost the business. Dad couldn't find another job that paid enough for him to make house payments, and they'd been forced to move to a much smaller place. That was when Grace's father had changed.

From Grace's twelfth birthday until the day

she and her mom left to come back to Missouri, now Brennans instead of Babcocks, she remembered so few good times with either of her parents. Her mom forgot how to smile, and she warned Grace repeatedly about losing herself in a relationship. For a couple of years after moving to Missouri, she didn't allow Grace to date.

Things lightened up after Grace graduated from high school. As her mom began to heal emotionally, she'd insisted that Grace get into counseling.

Grace had refused.

Now she couldn't help wondering if, somewhere in her subconscious, her mom's warnings had combined with personal experience to lock a door inside her that might never open.

Delight's smile cracked around the edges as she watched Denton's profile. The man never smiled anymore. And his constant conflict with Ladonna over songs made everybody crazy. Especially Delight.

Even after the way she'd treated him, he continued to push for her to have more exposure. Why?

And worse, because he continued to show

her so much partiality, no one in the cast respected her.

As conversations drifted across the table without her, she saw Grace get up and stroll over to the window, as if suddenly fascinated by the darkening shapes of the tree-covered hills. Michael's gaze followed her every movement.

What would it be like to have that kind of man love you that much?

She glanced sideways at Blake, who was listening to Cassidy describe his morning job as a surgery tech. So that was where Cassidy got the extra money for those fancy clothes he loved to wear, the flashy jewelry, the Escalade he drove.

She studied Cassidy as he laughed a little more loudly than usual, then glanced at his drink glass. He'd been to the Library Lounge at least a couple of times. Looked as if he was drinking some hard stuff and having a good time.

"Wish I could land a contract with a recording company from Nashville," Cassidy muttered. "At least *I* wouldn't make them wait for a decision."

"Who wouldn't like a contract?" Blake

asked. "But wishing doesn't make it so. I'm just going to focus on being the best I can be."

Cassidy shot a resentful look toward Grace's back as she stood at the window looking out. "She doesn't play fair."

Delight felt a trickle of guilt. *She* hadn't exactly been playing fair lately, and her jealousy of Grace had been much like Cassidy's.

The thought suddenly made her sick. She excused herself from the table.

Elegant desserts graced each place setting and the aroma of after-dinner coffee lingered in the air when the headwaiter approached Grace with the check. She gave him her charge card, glanced past his left shoulder and caught sight of Jolene Tucker sitting down in Delight's empty chair as Michael's expression took on the look of a cornered animal.

"Oh, please, Grace," Mitzi hissed, "tell me you didn't invite that woman here tonight."

"You know better, but I couldn't very well tell Denton who to date."

"You think he's been feeding her that information all along?" Ladonna asked.

"I've given up trying to figure it out."

Sherilyn chuckled. "Grace *should* be spilling her guts to Jolene. It's called exposure."

"Why can't it be good exposure?" Ladonna asked. "Why can't that woman write about the time Grace donates at the soup kitchen in Springfield or that Michael volunteers at the homeless shelter?"

"Nobody wants to read about the sweet, sappy stuff," Sherilyn said. "They want dirt, and plenty of it. That's what sells, and Jolene knows that."

"She's still a gossip," Mitzi muttered.

Sherilyn pushed her chair back, pasted on a smile and went to Michael's rescue.

Just then the headwaiter approached Grace and asked to speak with her privately. She got up and followed him through a door at the far end of the room into an office.

The headwaiter gestured for her to have a chair, then sat down across from her and held out her charge card. "I'm sorry, ma'am, but there's a problem with this."

She frowned down at it. "A problem?"

"It was rejected."

"But that can't be possible." She had a high limit on that card, and she paid off her balance every month.

"We ran it through three times." He hesitated, obviously embarrassed. "Sometimes these things happen. Perhaps there's been an error, but I called the company and was told you had already reached your limit."

"Then they must have made some mistake. Did they say what else was supposedly charged against it?"

"No, I'm sorry, but you're welcome to use our telephone to call the company yourself. Of course, we'll have no trouble extending you our own credit if you—"

"No, that won't be necessary. I can write you a check."

"That would be fine."

Then she realized she'd changed purses, and hadn't brought her checkbook with her. Just great.

So she took the headwaiter up on his offer and used the phone, hoping to clear up the error and pay with the credit card after all. But instead she discovered something shocking.

The Lladró had been charged to her.

Delight stepped out of the ladies' room downstairs and paused. She usually loved parties, but lately she'd been enjoying things less and worrying more.

Instead of returning upstairs immediately, she strolled through the atrium, where a waterfall splashed into a pool behind an ornate wooden railing.

She didn't want to turn out like Cassidy, whom no one took seriously because he was about as deep as a birdbath. And yet she'd been so focused on herself lately that she hadn't realized she was quickly becoming another publicity scrambler—one of those entertainers so desperate for the spotlight, for personal praise and adoration, that they didn't have a life. They scrambled to every audition they could find, fawned over the stars, made sure to be at the right place at the right time to catch the right person's attention. They used people to advance their careers. In the end, did they enjoy any of it?

"I'm not like that," she whispered toward the stream that trickled beneath the bridge on which she stood. "Am I?"

She had set goals for herself. There was nothing wrong with setting goals. She wanted to be a successful Branson entertainer. The world needed entertainment.

She heard footsteps on the stairs behind her, and she strolled past tables and chairs and a bank of elevators toward a waterfall that splashed into a meandering pool.

"Delight." A deep voice came from behind her.

She froze and closed her eyes. Denton.

"Are you okay?"

She nodded as she stepped to the railing and leaned against it. *Be nice and maybe he'll go away.* "No problem here—just enjoying the water. It kind of reminds me of Bass Pro up in Springfield. You know the wildlife place on the corner of Sunshine and Campbell?"

"Yes. Nice place." He stepped up beside her. "I like a good hike in the woods better."

"Not me," Delight said. "I like the climate control."

He leaned against the railing next to her, and she could smell the spicy scent of his aftershave. "I'd intended to have this talk with you under different circumstances, but it looks as if this is the best I'm going to get."

She turned to leave, and he placed a hand on her arm.

"Delight, we're going to have this talk, even if we have to air a great deal of dirty laundry at the table upstairs." His eyes narrowed as he continued to hold her arm and look down at her.

Her shoulders slumped as she relented.

He gestured to a nearby table with two chairs, then pulled out one of the chairs for her. "Just hear me out, then I'll leave you alone if you still want me to. I promise."

She glanced longingly up the stairs, then did as she was asked. He sat down across from her. The splash of the water provided a barrier so passersby would not hear them.

"Do you remember I told you about doing things I later regretted?" he asked.

"Yes." She heard the resentful sound of her own voice.

"I graduated from high school with honors, and had a full scholarship to SMSU in Springfield. But by the time I completed my second year, I had become quite an entrepreneur in the specialty coffee business, and I decided I didn't have time for college."

"Looks like you did pretty good for yourself."

"That isn't the end of the story. Four years after I quit college, I met a girl and fell in love. Eventually she decided that without a degree I wouldn't truly amount to anything, so she married someone else. I could have sworn she loved me, but she apparently preferred a man with a higher education."

"So you never finished college?"

"Yes, I did. Because of her, I returned to

school later and completed my education with a degree in business administration."

"So you're trying to tell me to finish college?" she asked. "Is that what this is all about?"

"Would you let me finish? There's another point to this story. I kept tabs on this woman through some business connections, and discovered she and her new husband had a baby girl two months after they were married. I also discovered that she hadn't even known her husband when she became pregnant."

"You *stalked* her?" Delight fought the urge to get up immediately and escape this man. "Did you keep a picture of her in your room, too?"

He closed his eyes and sighed. "Delight, you can be one of the rudest and most obtuse—"

"Okay, I'm sorry, but there seems to be a pattern here."

He glowered at her. "That was *my* baby. I know it was, because I did the math." A tremor of bitterness threaded his voice. "Our relationship had been an exclusive one, if you know what I mean."

"I wish I didn't. Why are you telling me this?"

"Hear me out. I contacted the woman and

asked if I could see the baby, and told her I knew I was the father." His voice caught, and he paused before he continued. "I wanted to pay child support, to be a part of the little girl's life. She refused. I stopped short of forcing a paternity suit."

Delight felt a very unwilling tug of compassion for this man with the tired, lined face and suddenly trembling voice.

"That baby was born twenty years ago," he said.

There was no way for Delight to misread the tenderness with which he said the words. "So your daughter must be my age." Okay, so maybe there was a reason he'd taken a special interest in her. Could it be he was reaching out to her because he couldn't be with his own child? "Why don't you approach her now that she's grown up and old enough to make her own decisions?"

Denton's brows shot up. He leaned back in his chair. "That's exactly what I'm doing."

Delight froze. All the oxygen seemed to leave the air and Denton's face grew fuzzy. She refused to faint. For a moment she couldn't open her mouth, for fear she might start screaming and never stop.

But this was crazy! "You can't be trying to tell me..."

"I don't make a fool of myself over a woman young enough to be my daughter unless she *is* my daughter."

Delight opened her mouth, then closed it. The noise of the waterfall behind them became a roar in her ears. "Why didn't you tell me sooner?" she asked at last. "How do you know I'm your daughter? And how do I know you're not making this up?"

"Ask your mother."

"I can't." She would not do that to her mom.

But if this was true, how could her mom do this to *her*? How could her *dad* do this to her? "You've known me all this time and you haven't said anything to me before this?"

"Think about it for a minute, Delight. It isn't something one just blurts out without preparation." He glanced toward the waterfall irritably, as if he, too, found the noise distracting. "I'd hoped we could build some kind of relationship before I dumped this heavy knowledge on you."

"That obviously didn't work," she muttered.

"This has probably been the hardest thing I've ever done. I've struggled with thoughts of the possible consequences from the time you first auditioned for the show."

"You knew who I was *then?*"

"Of course I knew. I've kept track of you ever since you were born. Even though your mother refused to acknowledge me, I wasn't about to let my only child be taken out of my life completely."

"You sure you've got the right person? My family lives in Alabama."

"Your mother attended SMSU in Springfield, Missouri, and she's always been fascinated by Branson. You vacationed here from time to time when you were growing up. Isn't that why you decided to attend college here?"

She closed her eyes against the impact of his words. Why hadn't they told her?

A drifting thought occurred to her. "Is that why I have this job?"

He looked away.

She braced her elbows on the table and buried her face in her hands. She hadn't been selected for her voice or her dancing abilities or any other talent. She'd been selected because of who she knew—or rather, because of who knew her...or thought he knew her.

Was it possible he truly was crazy? He'd made some dandy blunders the past few weeks. Now this guy thought he was her father! Was he really?

What about the man she had loved as her own daddy all these years? He'd never let on, never treated her any differently from the way he treated her brothers.

"Your mother came to Missouri from a well-to-do family in Montgomery, Alabama, and fell for the wrong man," Denton said. "That man wore down her defenses until she was unable to resist him, and she lived to regret those nights of passion."

Delight was going to throw up. She didn't want to hear this.

"She chose to marry a man from her hometown, someone her parents approved of, whom she believed could support her and a family comfortably. Not a college dropout."

Voices reached them from the top of the stairs, and Ladonna and Mitzi came down. Instead of heading straight toward the restrooms, they chose this uncomfortable moment to take a tour of the waterfall and bridge and pools. They caught sight of Denton and Delight, then dropped their gazes and hurried past. Delight wanted to follow them and get away from this man.

"I don't believe you," she whispered once

the others stepped out of earshot. "I think you're crazy." She couldn't look at him. She shoved her chair back and stood. She had to get out of there.

"Delight, ask your mother," he called after her.

She reached the stairs and raced away from him.

Chapter Sixteen

Grace strained at the highest note of "Party in Heaven." Her voice cracked. Frustrated, she broke off and turned to ask the band to start from the top, but another voice continued where hers ended.

Delight caught her attention with a brief smile and a nod of her head as she sang. Phoebe and Rachel harmonized.

Grace reached for the water bottle at her feet, exhausted, frustrated, mystified. Her mouth felt filled with cotton. Again. In spite of the copious amounts of water she drank.

She nodded in approval at the heavenly sound as the three women finished the song. "That works," she croaked.

"But what's up with you?" Delight asked,

giving Grace a quick look of concern as she stepped down from the riser.

Ladonna stepped up onto the stage from the first row of seats, perspiration dampening the curls of black hair that fell into her face. "Grace, are you okay?"

"What's going on down there?" Denton's clipped words came from far above them, where the window to Henry's old office overlooked the auditorium. "They're taping our show tonight for the television pilot."

"I know that." Grace took another swallow of water, then held the bottle against her face to cool down.

"Maybe the stress is getting to her," Cassidy said.

"After two years of live shows?" Delight snorted. "I doubt it. Sounds like laryngitis to me. Grace, you sick? Hope you didn't give it to me."

Grace's new cell phone chose that moment to announce, in a sultry, feminine voice, that she had an incoming call. She knew it was against the rules for them to take calls during practice. With Mom on a buying trip, however, Grace wanted to be available for her—a leftover sentiment from the "you-and-me-against-the-world" mentality in which Grace had spent the last half of her teen years.

She gave Ladonna an apologetic look.

Ladonna glanced toward Denton, who continued to stand at the open window to his new office, glaring down at them.

"Take a break," she said. "But only about ten minutes. Grace, go gargle or something. You picked a rotten time to be sick."

"I'm not sick." Grace shot the words over her shoulder as she stepped from the stage. She couldn't be sick.

She checked the caller ID screen on her cell phone and almost pressed it off without answering. It was Sherilyn. On impulse, however, she connected.

"Can I call you later?" she said quickly, forcing her voice past the sizable bullfrog that seemed to have taken her tonsils captive in the past thirty minutes. "We're practicing."

"Hey, doll, you sound like you've swallowed sandpaper," came the sultry-deep voice of her agent.

"I know that. Look, can I—"

"This won't take but a minute. Sweetie, you're a genius, but you should've talked to me about your publicity program first."

Grace sighed. She should have known

Sherilyn wouldn't be put off so easily. "What are you talking about?"

"All I'm saying is I could've helped so it wouldn't all turn to mush like this. Our dear Jolene wouldn't have guessed—"

"Hold it." Grace glanced over her right shoulder at the curious faces of the backup singers. Sherilyn's voice carried well, and this wasn't a good time for an exposé.

With a wave of apology Grace excused herself and retreated to the quick-change room just offstage. "Do you mind telling me what you're talking about?" she said when she closed the door.

"The publicity stunt. The music boxes, the Lladró, the threats? You definitely got the public's attention, but I could have kept Jolene from catching on so—"

"Publicity stunt? You've got to be kidding. You think all that was something I did for publicity? Come on, Sherilyn."

"Honey, it's all over the papers, and I imagine it'll be a major write-up in *Across the Country* this weekend. Jolene won't be able to resist something this juicy."

Grace's light-headedness suddenly hit her with renewed force. "What kind of juicy are you talking about?" She raised the water bottle to her lips for a long swig that didn't break the power of thirst or wet the cotton in her mouth. What an awful day.

"It's right here in the local paper," Sherilyn said. "A major story about how those gifts were charged to your own account."

Grace choked on the water. "Oh, of all the ridiculous things…Sherilyn, you know me better than that. You can't honestly think I'd do something like that."

Silence on the other end of the line.

"Hello?"

"I called the horse's mouth," Sherilyn said at last.

"What horse's mouth? Stop talking in riddles."

"Jolene Tucker. She's the one who did the story in the local paper."

"You called her?"

"You got that right, baby. Seems she's been doing some freelance work the past week or so. Anyway, it was her byline. I was in the process of teaching her the libel laws until she told me she had proof."

"What kind of proof?"

"Her mole sent her a copy of your credit-card bill. It's right there in plain English, Grace. Those gifts were charged to your account."

"I'm aware of that, and I've already had a nice long talk with representatives from the company."

"And?"

"And I've already returned the gifts and had the charges reversed, but I didn't do the charging in the first place. It's called identity theft, in case you've never heard of it."

There was another silence, then Sherilyn said, "You sure about that?"

"Positive. I've already called the police. How did Jolene's mole get a copy of my credit-card bill? That's invasion of privacy. Maybe I'll need to make another call to the police." Grace's voice had nearly disappeared.

"Okay, if you didn't do it, who did? And why?"

"How am I supposed to know?" Grace took another swallow of water. Something was definitely wrong with her. The voice just refused to work. Period. Delight might get her wish and take on the whole show if this continued.

"I'll tell you who it looks like to me," Sherilyn said. "Who's suddenly buddies with Jolene?"

"You mean Denton?" Grace croaked. "A bit obvious, don't you think?"

"Sure it's obvious, but it isn't as if the man has a reason to hide what he's doing. This is publicity, Grace. It's like I've been telling you all along. You've got the public eye, so milk it for all it's worth."

Grace rolled her eyes. Sherilyn and her clichés. "Have you ever milked a cow?"

"I grew up in east St. Louis. What do you think?"

"I milked some goats for a friend of mine in Hideaway," Grace said. "When those goats go dry, there's no more milk. I'm about to go dry, so they're scrabbling for nonexistent information."

Sherilyn groaned. "Honey, that is not a pretty picture to leave me with."

"Sorry. Can I hang up now? The cast is likely to become Branson's latest lynch mob if I don't get back out there."

Michael carried a large plastic cup of his special brew to the quick-change room, where he'd seen Grace enter.

The door opened, and she stood on the threshold looking like warmed-over dinner from a week ago. "What's up?" she whispered.

"You're sick."

"I can't be."

"So tell me how you're feeling."

She fingered perspiration from her forehead and eased herself onto the padded dressing bench. Slowly. As if she was dizzy. But would she admit that to him? No.

"Stupid and frustrated," she said. "Jolene caught wind of what happened the other night at the Chateau."

He stared at her blankly. "What happened at the Chateau, other than the fact that Denton brought the wolf into the sheep's pen, and Delight returned from the bathroom begging Blake to take her home immediately without any explanation?"

Grace sighed. "I'm sorry. Of course you wouldn't know." She patted the seat beside her. "I forgot you never read the paper. My credit card was rejected, so I had to arrange for credit with the Chateau."

"So? Jolene must've been scraping for news if she—"

"I discovered the reason my card was rejected. The Lladró I received last week was charged to my account." Her voice broke with hoarseness. "My credit-card company doesn't call to verify large purchases the way some do."

He sank down beside her. Hard. "No way."

She nodded. "Someone definitely found a way, because I sure didn't do it."

He had no doubt about that. But who would have been in a position to do this? "Do you do much shopping on the Internet?"

She shook her head. "Never with that card."

"Are you still refusing to call the police?"

"I called, and they're taking care of things as discreetly as possible. Unfortunately, when they asked the music box companies and delivery companies who paid them, guess what their answer was."

"You?"

"You got it."

He glanced at his watch. No time for this talk right now. He handed her the cup. "Drink this."

She gazed down into the red liquid. "What is it?"

"My own special vitamin C concoction for emergencies. It's dissolved in tepid water, just the right temperature. I could kick myself for not starting you on it earlier, but I didn't want you to have to make any decisions about trust when you have so much to worry about."

She took the cup from him as she gave him a level look. "Did you think I'd accuse you of trying to poison me?"

He grimaced. "Sorry. I didn't mean that the way it sounded. So trust me and drink it all."

She tasted it and wrinkled her nose. "Sour."

"Drink."

She did as she was told and handed the empty cup back to him. "Think it'll help?"

"At this point, nothing could hurt."

"Michael Gold, the hopeless optimist," she drawled with whispered sarcasm.

"I'll get some more." He got up and reached for the door.

"Michael?"

He turned back. She looked so vulnerable, her face so pale. His heart flipped a double rhythm in his chest as he looked into those lovely and beloved eyes.

"Do you think I bought those gifts and wrote those notes myself for publicity?" she asked.

He grinned. "Everybody's embarrassingly aware of the way you court the press." He hoped his sarcasm surpassed her own. "You love being the center of attention."

Her expression seemed to relax, and those aquamarine eyes glowed with sudden warmth. "Sherilyn thinks I did it."

"Sherilyn doesn't know you as well as I do, does she?"

"Obviously you know me better than I know you."

"Maybe that's partially my fault," he said.

"Oh, really?"

"I said partially."

"I know you better than you think," she said. "And I trust you more than it shows, obviously."

"Save your voice."

She nodded. "The problem is me, Michael."

He had thought about that a lot the past couple of weeks. "I've never been betrayed by someone on whom I was dependent," he said softly. "I think trust would be a major challenge for me if I had been."

She looked down at the cell phone in her hands. "You know the day I freaked and walked out on you at the restaurant?" she whispered.

She was kidding, right? "Vaguely."

"I was upset because I'd hurt you."

"We were both upset that day. I think we both said some things we didn't necessarily mean. And if you keep talking, you'll lose your voice completely."

She placed her cell phone on the bench beside her and stood up. She swayed.

He reached for her. "Grace, have you taken

some new medication? Please tell me you aren't taking diet pills of any kind. You've been losing weight far too quickly."

She frowned at him. "No drugs." But she allowed him to steady her, and she didn't complain when his hands remained on her arms. "Michael, just before I met you that day, I discovered my father was trying to contact me. Combined with my concerns about the nasty notes, it all became too much. I'm sorry." Her voice was nearing a whisper again.

Her eyes looked strange.

Michael tipped her chin up and studied her pupils. They were dilated, her skin was hot and perspiration moistened her forehead in spite of the air-conditioned coolness of the room.

And then her words registered. "Your father?"

She nodded, her eyes searching his as if waiting for an answer to a question she hadn't asked. He got the distinct impression he was supposed to be reading her mind right now.

"Have you spoken with him?" he asked.

She shook her head.

At least she was attempting to heed his

warning about voice rest. "And you're asking *my* advice?"

"About forgiveness," she croaked.

Ouch. He released her chin and turned away. "I'm not exactly a shining example of that virtue."

"But you've forgiven me, haven't you?"

He nodded. He couldn't stay angry with Grace.

"You're sure?"

He turned back to her. "I'm sure."

"How did you forgive me?"

"I prayed about it, and I realized that forgiveness is a process of steps. The first step is to acknowledge that refusal to forgive is a sin. That's a truth from the Bible. A person can't make a truth go away just because he doesn't want to see it. It's like seeing a rattlesnake in the grass and deciding it isn't there. The thing is still dangerous."

"So thinking about rattlesnakes helped you decide to forgive me?"

He grinned as he held up the cup. "Wait right here. You need some more of this."

Delight found the courage to call her mother just before show time Thursday night. She waited until she knew the man she'd always called Daddy would be at his deacons' meeting.

When her mother answered, Delight almost got cold feet and disconnected.

"Honey?" Mom said. "What's wrong? Shouldn't you be in a show?" She had caller ID.

"In a few minutes. I just needed to…um… ask you a question."

"Well, sure, but can I call you back on my cell phone? I've got to take your brothers to a party at church, and if they're late, they'll never let me —"

"Just a quick question, Mom. It's all I have time for." Delight the coward. "Did I ever tell you about the guy who owns the theater here?"

There was a short silence. "That's the question you wanted to ask just before a show?"

Delight knew from the sound of her mother's voice that she suspected something. "You know him?"

This time, no answer.

"His name is Denton Mapes." Delight heard the quiver in her own voice.

There was a long pause, then a heavy, drawn-out sigh. "Yes."

Delight raised a trembling hand to her lips.

No. Oh, no, no, no! "H-how long have you known he was the owner of the theater where I worked?"

Another awkward pause. "Really, honey, this isn't a good time. I need to—"

"Please just tell me this—is he...did you know him in college?"

There was a sharp gasp over the line. "He *told* you?"

Delight squeezed her eyes tightly shut. It was true. A shaft of nearly physical pain shot through her. Her daddy wasn't really her father? And they'd never told her?

"Oh, Jesus, help me," she whispered. It was the first prayer she'd prayed in a long time.

"Delight?" her mom said softly. "Honey, we need to talk."

"I'll see you at Christmas, Mom. I know all I need to know." She hung up, her face wet with tears.

It was true—Denton Mapes was her father!

And her mom had never warned her, never given any hint. How could she deceive Delight so?

And yet there was no time to even think about this now. She needed a quick makeup repair before the curtain came up.

Sniffing and wiping her eyes, she cut

through a seldom-used storage area that was off-limits to cast and crew, but she needed a shortcut to the dressing rooms. Deep in the shadows she tripped over a concrete block, stumbled against a ladder and muttered under her breath.

She was bent down, rubbing her leg, when she caught sight of Cassidy Ryder carrying an armload of water bottles through the dim light. He apparently drank the same brand as Grace.

As Delight followed him at a distance, he stopped at Grace's stash, removed the bottles already there and replaced them with the new ones.

Cassidy Ryder, water boy. How weird was that?

Grace thanked God for the power of prayer and an extra dose of adrenaline as her voice carried her through the second stanza of the final song before intermission. The theater was filled almost to capacity, and the response to their show tonight continued to be enthusiastic. The audiences still loved the interactive byplay.

That potion Michael had forced her to drink had worked wonders, at least for a while. But the relief hadn't lasted. Now she felt awful. But she couldn't let on, even though the heat from the spotlights made her perspire heavily, which in turn made her fear for her carefully applied makeup job.

She glanced at the band over her shoulder and winked at Michael, who sang from his position at the piano keyboard. When he returned the wink she swung back around to face the audience.

She stumbled as her right foot wobbled on the high heel, and she nearly turned her ankle.

Stepping to the edge of the stage, she waved and applauded with the rest of the cast as they showed their genuine appreciation for their beloved supporters.

But tonight, for some reason, those cherished faces blurred as she waved to them.

Grace turned, still clapping, and realized she couldn't feel the impact of her hands against each other. She couldn't feel her feet as she walked across the stage.

The heat increased, and the faces in the audience became a blur. The theater began to spin around her in a nauseating merry-go-round of sound and lights.

She opened her mouth to sing the final stanza, and nothing came out. She swallowed and licked her lips, but before she could try again, another voice, clear and high, merged with perfect symmetry to the music.

Grace turned with dizzying swiftness to find Delight, Phoebe and Rachel harmonizing without her. She smiled, but as she moved toward them, her feet refused to cooperate. She stumbled and fell.

She tried to get back up, but a heavy weight pressed her onto the stage. Darkness overwhelmed her. The sound, the hardness of the floor and the lights all receded as blackness caught her up into nothingness.

Michael scrambled from the piano bench and raced across the stage. "Grace!"

Her face glowed pale in the spotlight, and he pressed his fingers to her carotid artery.

He froze. Nothing. No pulse. "Somebody call 9-1-1!"

Chapter Seventeen

Michael paced the small confines of the family conference room at the hospital, frantic to hear news of Grace. This place resembled the green room at the theater before a performance, with half the cast in attendance, sitting on chairs and sofa and even the floor as they waited for the doctor to break free and talk with Grace's mother.

"What's takin' them so long?" Delight fidgeted on a straight-back chair at the far side of the room.

"No news means good news at this point," Michael said, hoping it was true.

No, he didn't just hope. He prayed. *Oh, God, please protect her. Bring her back to us. I can't bear the thought of losing her, and if that's selfish of me, I'm sorry. If You take*

*her from us now, think of all the people who
will miss the loving testimony of her music.*

He sat down next to Grace's mother and
heard the raggedness of her breathing. The
tips of Kathryn Brennan's fingers whitened
as she gripped her hands together.

Peter sat on the floor by the wall next to
Delight, legs crossed. Blake sat on Delight's
other side, and Denton huddled by the door
next to an openly weeping Mitzi. Phoebe and
Rachel had stayed at the theater with Cassidy
and Ladonna to make sure the guests made
it out safely and everything was left in order.

"It's been thirty minutes," Kathryn said.

Michael put a comforting hand on her
shoulder and squeezed. "I'm sure they're trying to stabilize her. Just keep praying."

Across the room Delight bowed her head
and closed her eyes, her lips moving silently
as tears slipped down her cheeks. Blake put
an arm around her. Denton watched her with
obvious concern.

"Michael, can't you go in there and hurry
things up?" Peter asked. "You're practically
a doctor."

"I'm not a doctor, I don't work here and we
have to give them room to—"

The door opened, and Kathryn caught her

breath. A harried-looking man who appeared to be in his late thirties stepped into the room, wearing scrubs and a white lab coat with a badge. Michael recognized the name. He'd visited Cheyenne at Hideaway Clinic a couple of times.

"Hello," the man said. "I'm Dr. Gordon Renneker, and I've been taking care of Ms. Brennan. Is there family here? I need to get as much information as quickly as I can."

Kathryn leaned forward. "I'm her mother. These people all work with her, and they were with her when she collapsed. How is she?"

Dr. Renneker perched on the arm of the sofa. "Her condition is critical but stable. Who can tell me exactly what happened?"

"She collapsed onstage," Michael said. "I went to her immediately, and she had no pulse." He nodded toward Delight. "We did CPR and rescue breathing until the paramedics arrived."

"Congratulations," Dr. Renneker said. "Your fast action may have saved her life."

Kathryn caught her breath and leaned weakly against Michael. He felt a little weak himself.

"She was sick before that, though," Delight said. "She stumbled a couple of times, and

she was havin' a lot of trouble with her voice.
It kept goin' out on her, even in practice, remember, Michael?"

The doctor nodded. "That coincides with
our findings. She probably would have had
dry mouth. She had a high fever. Is she aller-
gic to anything?"

"Penicillin," Kathryn said. "Nothing else
I know of."

"Does she take any medications regularly?"
he asked.

"Only vitamins." Kathryn looked up at
Michael. "Isn't that right? She wasn't taking
anything for her laryngitis, was she?"

"No. I asked her this afternoon during a
break in practice. She wasn't taking anything.
She had no known health problems except for
her recent trouble with hoarseness."

Dr. Renneker frowned. "How long has the
hoarseness been going on?"

Michael looked at Grace's mother. "At least
a few weeks, wouldn't you say?"

"That's right," Kathryn said. "Doctor, what
do her symptoms suggest?"

He gave a baffled shake of his head. "At
first glance, if I were to take a guess, it appears
to be some kind of anticholinergic poisoning."

"She was *poisoned?*" Peter exclaimed.

"I'm talking about a drug that speeds things up in the body and can have bad effects on the heart," the doctor explained, his dark, heavy brows forming a V across his forehead. "It would have triggered a lethal arrhythmia."

"Did you do a blood test?" Michael asked.

"Yes, and it was negative, which might only mean our lab isn't set up for whatever might be in the blood. Fortunately, there's a treatment for that class of poisoning, but it would really help to know what she's ingested, if anything."

"But she wouldn't take anything like that," Kathryn protested, her slender hands spread in the air helplessly.

"Just in case, though," Dr. Renneker said, "it would help us if someone would go through her purse or her medicine cabinet at home and see if there's anything we might be missing. If you say she's had trouble with hoarseness, it's possible she's been taking something she doesn't realize could be causing her trouble."

"Like what?" Kathryn asked.

"Diet pills, perhaps?" the doctor suggested.

"I asked her that tonight," Michael said. "She hasn't been."

"Maybe something else that might otherwise seem innocuous?" the doctor asked. "If you find any kind of cold care product or prescription bottle, something she might have been taking, bring it in or call us." He rose from his perch on the sofa arm. "If you'll forgive me, I need to get back in there."

"Please," Kathryn said softly, "can I see her?"

The doctor moved toward the door. "I'm sorry, ma'am, but that wouldn't be wise. She isn't out of danger yet, and we might have to take drastic measures at any moment. She's still not totally conscious, and she has a tube down her throat to help her breathe. I'll keep you informed as we find out more."

"Doctor, are you saying Grace could still die?"

Dr. Renneker hesitated, then nodded gravely. "I'm sorry, I have to get back in there."

As the doctor left the room, Kathryn buried her face in her hands. Michael put his arm around her. *Oh, Lord, please protect Grace.*

Delight wanted to wake up from this awful nightmare. Poisoning? What if Grace really did die? This couldn't be happening.

"Well, what now?" Peter asked, getting to his feet. "Want me to go to the theater and search through her stuff?"

Delight jumped to her feet. "If you do, I'm going with you." The big, clumsy bozo wouldn't know what to look for, and wouldn't recognize it if it bit him.

Mitzi stood. "I'll drive to her condo if someone will give me a key."

"Wait." Kathryn grabbed her purse and stood. "I should be the one to go to Grace's place. I know where everything is. But I'm telling you, we won't find a thing. We all know she'll barely take an aspirin for a headache. Even with that blasted laryngitis, she'd barely use throat spray for fear it would mess up her voice."

"Maybe we're missing an important point," Peter said. "The doc said she was poisoned. Poisoning's something that's *done* to a person, right? Not something they do themselves."

"That's just a medical term," Michael said.

Peter crossed his arms over his chest. "Okay, smarty, then are you going to tell me Grace really has been sending herself those gifts and threatening messages? Because to me, it just seems like there might be some danger involved there. Somebody who would threaten her might follow through on it."

The room grew silent as the two men locked gazes. Delight felt a niggle at the back of her mind. What was she missing?

She glanced at Denton. Who was he, really? What lengths would he go to for his daughter if he really wanted to help her in her career? And what about Mitzi? Could she be that vindictive over a simple embarrassment weeks ago?

Kathryn reached for Michael's arm. "What if Peter's right? Grace kept trying to dismiss those notes as some kind of prank or publicity stunt, but I've been worried about her ever since this whole mess began. Someone had access to her credit card. What else did they have access to?"

"Somebody really could be poisoning her?" Blake asked.

"That's crazy," Denton said. "Stop grasping for straws and find out what's really going on."

"No, wait a minute, maybe someone's been slippin' something into her food, or…" Delight caught her breath and sat up straight. "Oh, her water! I saw Cassidy hauling an armload of water bottles to the stage tonight, and he replaced hers with the ones he was carrying. At the time I just thought he was being nice and replacing her used ones, but he did glance over his shoulder as if checking to see if anyone saw him doing it. What if—"

"What if there's something in that water." Michael's face suddenly lost some color. "Her doctor recommended she change brands, so she stopped drinking her own brand of bottled water a couple of weeks ago and started drinking from the community cooler until she could buy a different brand. When she drank from the cooler for a few days I didn't hear her complain one time about her throat."

"Are you saying Cassidy Ryder might have poisoned Grace?" Denton asked, rising from his seat at last.

"I'm sayin' it's a possibility we'd better not ignore." Delight pushed her chair aside and joined Denton at the door.

"Think about poor old Henry," Peter said. "Everybody says he died of natural causes, but what if someone did him in, too?"

"Think Cassidy could find something from

the operating room to poison Grace?" Blake asked. "He's a scrub tech, remember?"

"And Cassidy resented Grace," Delight said. "He'd said a few things about her manufacturing her own breaks and not playing fair."

"Cassidy Ryder, of course!" Mitzi said. "Michael, remember the day I told you and Grace about the fight I overheard between Henry and someone else? Later on, after they decided Henry died of natural causes, I remembered walking out into the parking lot that day and seeing a carload of teenagers nearly clip the front fender of Cassidy's Escalade. That means he was in the theater somewhere at the time. He might've been the one Henry was fighting with."

"What were they fighting about?" Denton asked.

"Something about nose jobs and recognizing faces and having a long memory," Mitzi said. "I didn't understand it."

"Henry mentioned something like that the night he chewed everybody out," Blake said. "Remember? When he told Cassidy to straighten out his act, he said, 'Ryder—or whatever you're calling yourself these days.' I remember it struck me odd, because we didn't know Cassidy had a stage name."

Peter snorted. "You mean like Blake Montana?"

"Hey," Blake said, "I was born in Montana, okay? My agent suggested it."

"So what's your real name?"

"Could we get back to the subject?" Michael pulled his billfold from his pocket and took a card from it. He handed it to Kathryn. "You have a cell phone, don't you?"

She took the card and looked at it. "You want me to call the police?"

"That's the number of the detective who questioned me on Henry's case. You stay here and wait to see Grace, but call this woman. Tell her what we suspect about the poisonings, and send her with a cavalry to the theater. I'm going to find out if Cassidy's still there." Since the hospital was so close to the theater, he had a chance to beat the police there.

He suddenly remembered his conversation with Grace the same night that Henry had made the crack about Cassidy's identity. Who *was* Cassidy Ryder? And if he was who Michael suspected he might be, why had he suddenly flipped out again after all these years?

* * *

Michael pulled into the cast parking lot of the Classical Impressions Theater. The police had not yet arrived, but they would any moment. He couldn't be sure he'd find Cassidy here, even though the guy's SUV was parked in the far corner as usual, out of the high traffic area.

Ladonna met Michael in the lobby. "What's going on? Grace out of danger?"

"She's still in trouble," Michael said. "Have you seen Cassidy?"

"Sure. Last I saw him he was upstairs in Denton's office."

"You mean Henry's office."

Ladonna gave him a puzzled frown. "You know Denton's taken it over so he can monitor the show and nag us every time we get— hey, where are you going?"

Michael took the stairs two at a time. "I'm going to have a talk with Cassidy. Send the police up when they arrive."

When he reached the office he shoved the door open and burst into the room, where he found Cassidy sitting at the desk reading some sheet music.

Cassidy glanced up. "How's it going? Grace all right?"

Rage shot through Michael with frightening power, and he barely resisted the urge to leap the desk and grab the jerk by the shirt collar. "I'd have expected a little more concern than that. Most of the other cast members are either already at the hospital or are headed in that direction. I can't help wondering why you don't seem to care."

Cassidy dropped the sheet he'd been reading. "What's eating you?"

"Does the name Wes Reinhold mean anything to you?"

A flick of Cassidy's lids betrayed him. He swallowed, hesitating a little too long. "Should it?"

"Too bad we can't ask Henry that question. I hear Wes threatened to kill him once, years ago. Looks like maybe Henry did something to make him mad again, and this time good old Wes got the job done."

Cassidy slowly stood up from the desk where he had no right to be sitting in the first place. "Are you having an emotional crisis, Michael?" he asked softly.

"Not me. It's possible Henry had an emotional crisis and threatened his old acquaintance, though. Perhaps even to blackball him from Branson again? Or to expose him and ruin his career? Wes obviously has a temper problem."

"You're talking nonsense, Michael." Cassidy's voice was tight with tension.

Michael glanced at his watch. The police should be here any minute. "You know, it's difficult to work with people so closely day after day and not get to know them pretty well. In this case a few of us in the cast did some calculating and ended up with an interesting total."

"For instance?"

"You've had a special opportunity most of us general theater grunts don't have. You work in a surgical suite, with access to all kinds of wonder drugs that the surgeon uses to control his patients' bodily responses."

"So I'm special." Cassidy slid his hands into his pockets and leaned against the desk, obviously attempting to look casual.

"Special enough to think you have a right to poison a co-worker with one of those drugs?"

"Why would you even say such a thing? No one has that kind of right."

"I called a friend of mine on my way here,"

Michael said. "Ever heard of Nathan Trask? He's the pharmacist in Hideaway. We've been good friends for a lot of years."

"Is that supposed to impress me?" Cassidy asked.

"Maybe it should. Nathan told me about a drug that's used in surgery called glycopyrrolate." Michael watched Cassidy's face closely as a muscle clenched in the man's jaw. "It tends to dry the mucus membranes to keep a patient from salivating during surgery. It also tends to dry out the throat and can really mess up the voice of a singer, especially if that singer isn't aware of what's in her drinking water."

Some of the high color drained from Cassidy's face.

"It seems old Wes has been resurrected and wreaked some vengeance on some of his former foes," Michael said. "At least two of them."

Cassidy straightened from the desk and paced slowly to the window overlooking the theater. "Speculation doesn't catch a judge's attention."

"No, but it makes for some interesting discoveries," Michael said.

The window was open, and for a moment Michael thought Cassidy might close it. He didn't.

"You sent that first music box to her, didn't you?" Michael said. "What happened, Cassidy—did she beat you out of the contest Henry put on for amateurs all those years ago? So you threatened to expose her for cheating. But then you killed Henry. Exposing Grace could expose you. And then you decided to try to beat her out of the starring role by ruining her voice. Why didn't you slip that drug into *my* water? *I'm* the one in your way here on this show, not Grace. *I'm* the male lead."

Cassidy sighed and turned away from the window. "If I were going to harm someone— which, of course, I would never do—then you wouldn't be a good candidate. You're leaving the show after this season is over."

"And you know that because...?"

"I hear a lot when others aren't listening. I heard you calling Kirksville and setting up classes for the spring semester. You're going back to school."

Michael resisted the urge to yank Cassidy forward by the shirt collar and force further admission from him. "So you only meant to ruin her career, not kill her? Hurt her reputation with the bad publicity by telling Jolene about things you overheard here backstage? But it didn't hurt Grace's career."

Cassidy didn't reply.

"Then you realized the publicity was only helping Grace," Michael said. "So you took it a step further, found her personal information and charged the Lladró to her, then made sure Jolene discovered that dirty little bit of information."

Cassidy's gaze slid away from Michael. "Grace Brennan can do no wrong in this town."

"And you also poisoned her water with a drug you knew, from personal experience, would hurt her voice," Michael continued, his own voice trembling with fury.

"It never happened," Cassidy said.

"You were observed tampering with Grace's bottled water tonight." Michael took a step closer, forcing Cassidy to look at him. "Something you've obviously been doing for quite some time, injecting the drug into the bottles when she wasn't around." Michael wished he'd taken better notice the day Grace's bottle leaked before she even broke the seal on the lid. "Funny thing about that drug—it makes a person thirsty, and even as they drink, they get thirstier, especially when the very water they're drinking is laced with the stuff."

Cassidy smiled. "You're pretty smart, for a med school dropout." Before Michael realized what had happened, Cassidy stepped close. His hands came from his pockets, targeting Michael's throat.

Michael reached up to block him, but too late. He felt sharp pricks of pain on each side of his neck.

"See what happens when you lose your temper?" Cassidy growled. "Those jugulars become mighty prominent."

The pain raced down Michael's neck, and he choked and fell back. With the swiftness of flowing blood, weakness played havoc with his arms and legs. He glimpsed what Cassidy held in his hands—two yellow tubes that resembled portable epinephrine pens.

He'd received a double dose of pure adrenaline directly into his veins.

Cassidy grabbed Michael by the shirtsleeve and jerked him toward the window. Michael stumbled to a stop, but his responses weakened as his heart suddenly threatened to beat out of his chest.

Cassidy shoved Michael's head through the open window, giving him an unwanted glimpse of the catwalk a few yards down, and then farther, at the dangerous drop into the theater below.

"I didn't mean to risk Grace's life," Cassidy said. "I just wanted to see to it she didn't get all the breaks."

Michael tried to struggle, but the drug stayed his movements as if someone had poured thick, fast-acting glue over his limbs. It was the exact opposite of the response he would have expected. The double dose of epinephrine had combined with his natural adrenaline to overtax his heart.

"You could be tried for attempted murder," Michael said through lips that felt stiff and thick. "And if Grace dies, you could get Murder One."

"How are you feeling now, Michael?" Cassidy asked softly. "Feel like a little bungee jumping?"

Michael's ears roared with sound as he reluctantly turned his head and gazed at the theater seats far below.

Was this what Henry had faced? Cassidy

and his epi pens. If he'd used the same thing on Henry, it could easily have caused heart failure. That was why the autopsy suggested he had died of natural causes. Since epinephrine was adrenaline, no tests would have picked up on the excess in Henry's system.

Michael's own heart felt as if it would burst, breaking a few ribs in the process. He reached for the sill, but Cassidy grabbed his shoulders and shoved him hard through the window.

Michael's head whacked the top of the sill. He thrust his arms out to catch himself, but Cassidy shoved him again. Michael's hand snagged the windowsill for a precious few seconds, then he tumbled backward into empty air.

Before he could open his mouth to cry out, he landed on something solid. The breath burst from his lungs. The catwalk had stopped his fall.

Seconds later Cassidy landed beside him with the agility of a panther, then reached for Michael's shoulders. Michael scrambled backward. Cassidy followed and shoved again, this time harder.

Michael fell against the railing, and heard a sickening sound of cracking wood as the rail weakened with the impact of his body. Cassidy came at him like a charging bull and shoved with all his might. The railing broke away. Michael felt himself falling and reached up to snag the edge of the catwalk.

He caught a guide wire with his left hand, crying out as the wire tore into his flesh. Cassidy screamed as he went tumbling past Michael, his body arcing into the shadows.

Cassidy landed with an awful thud on the theater floor.

Grace grew aware of a tight stiffness in her throat, and of distant voices. She raised her hand to her throat and tried to call out, then gagged.

Gentle hands grasped hers. "It's okay, Grace. You're at the hospital and we have you intubated, so you can't talk, but it's helping you breathe."

She opened her eyes with difficulty, then winced at the brightness of the room. A doctor in a white coat stood over her, smiling. She tried to smile back, and gagged again.

"Relax for us, please. Everything's going to be okay. Your heart is stabilizing. You gave us quite a scare for a while."

She heard the sound of a heart monitor somewhere nearby.

"Grace, do you remember taking any kind of medication that might have given you this reaction?"

She reached for her throat again. She couldn't talk!

"Just blink once for yes, twice for no," the doctor said.

She blinked twice, wondering if the tube in her throat would damage her voice.

"It's good to see you back among the living," the doctor continued. "You're doing better. We were concerned we might have lost you earlier tonight."

Grace shot the doctor a startled look. She could have died? Without ever forgiving her father? Without ever telling Michael she loved him? Without accomplishing the things in her life that she felt God intended her to accomplish?

Oh, Lord, let me live. Let me make up for things I've left undone. Give me a chance to right some of my wrongs. She needed to tell the truth to her fans. Pride had kept her from it for so long. Time to come clean. Even if it meant nothing to anyone else, it meant something to her.

A new voice joined in as a dark-haired male nurse stepped beside the bed. "Your mother's about to break down the door to see you, and half your hometown and most of your fans have either descended on the waiting room or have the phone lines tied up. I hope you hurry up and recover, Ms. Brennan, because you're a handful to keep around here."

Grace blinked once. She wanted out, too.

Blake lay on his stomach and grasped Michael's left hand with both of his own. "Let go of the wire, Michael. Peter's here beside me. He'll grab your other hand and we'll get you up."

For a moment Michael hesitated, though he could see Peter lying on his stomach beside Blake, hands outstretched.

Other footsteps echoed on the catwalk as Michael's hand slid on the wire, slick with sweat and probably blood.

"Come on, man!" Blake said. "The police are coming up, but you're not going to hold on long enough for them to get here. You've got to let go."

Michael closed his eyes and said a silent prayer, then released the wire. He felt Peter's firm clasp, and gasped with pain as the two men pulled him to safety.

He kicked upward weakly and managed to roll onto the flat surface of the catwalk. "Cassidy?" His hands, legs and arms felt numb and rubbery. His head felt filled with helium.

"He's dead," Blake said softly.

Peter sniffed and wiped at his face with the back of his sleeve. "Broke his neck."

Michael stumbled to his feet and allowed the men to steady him. "He killed Henry. He poisoned Grace." This nightmare had to end. "We need to contact the hospital. Have you heard how she's doing?"

Blake guided him back along the catwalk. "Your buddy the pharmacist called the doctor and told him she might have ingested that glyco-whatever. I don't know what they did, but she's coming out of it."

Michael wobbled on the catwalk, and this time his weakness came from relief.

Chapter Eighteen

Grace felt overwhelmed by conflicting emotions as she sat alone on the chilly deck at Lakeside Bed and Breakfast in Hideaway the day after Christmas. On a low note, Cassidy had killed Henry and tried to kill Michael. All else paled in comparison, but he had also tried to ruin her career by poison and bad press.

On a good note, she'd been released from the hospital on Christmas Eve, at her insistence. She had attended a huge community Christmas dinner here in Hideaway, surrounded by loving and attentive friends.

On a questionable note, for the first time in her life she'd felt like a third wheel at her mom's house.

Malcolm and Kathryn had become good

friends as they nudged the threshold of romance. Though Grace cheered for her mother, she couldn't help wallowing in a little self-pity, and she felt like a heel about it. It was the first time she hadn't had her mother's undivided attention.

She would talk it all over with Michael this evening when he took her out to eat at Chateau on the Lake. She suspected he'd invited her simply to assure himself she was suffering no aftereffects of the drug, but she didn't care about that, only that she could spend time with him. She would have been content with a bologna sandwich right here on the deck.

First, however, she had an important call to make. After a long heart-to-heart with her old trusted friend Bertie, she thought she felt ready to take this next step of faith.

She pulled out her father's telephone number and spread the paper tightly across her knee to smooth the wrinkles. She slid her cell phone from her purse and punched in the numbers before she could back down.

Someone picked up after the second ring. "Hello?" The voice of a young child. Laughter echoed in the background, followed by the squeal of an apparently cranky infant.

"Hello," Grace said. "Is this Tyrel Babcock's residence?"

"That's my daddy. Who's this?"

Grace caught her breath. She was talking to her little sister. "I'm…my name's Grace Brennan, and I was wondering—"

"Grace Brennan!" There was a muffled clunk, as if the child had suddenly dropped the receiver, or tossed it onto a table. "Daddy! It's her! She *called!*"

With a sense of the surreal, Grace listened to her sister, Holly, chatter with excitement in the distance. Apparently her father didn't keep secrets from his new family.

A new voice came on the line—a deep voice she remembered even after all these years. "Grace?"

"Yes." She held her breath, bracing herself for a wash of confusing emotions—anger, fear, bitterness, pain.

And yet, after a night of sleeplessness and agonized prayers, she felt only sadness for something lost.

"Grace? It's really you? What a Christmas present!"

"I…would have called sooner, but…well, you've got to admit this is awkward."

"I didn't want to make you feel that way,"

he said gently. "All I really wanted to do was talk to you for a minute. I've spent years apologizing to God for what I did to you, unable to apologize to you face-to-face. I've been told I'll have to learn to forgive myself, but I can't do that until I have forgiveness from the person I hurt the worst."

Grace's hand gripped the cell phone. Her father had always gotten right to the point of a conversation. That, too, might be the reason she'd dreaded this call.

"Could be you're not ready for that," he said. "I probably wouldn't be if I were you."

"You don't believe in giving a person time to think about things, do you?"

"Take all the time you want."

She leaned her head back against the wall. Shouldn't there be more fanfare after all this time? Could this kind of forgiveness actually boil down to a simple question and a simple answer?

And yet, the most powerful forgiveness of all time boiled down to a simple turnaround, a genuine request for forgiveness, and a reply of love from the Father.

"Grace? Are you there?"

"I'm sorry. I've resented and feared you for so long, I don't know how we could possibly recover the relationship we once had." She winced at her own words. She hadn't meant to sound so harsh.

"I don't want that relationship. I'm not the same person I was then, and I'm sure you've done some changing yourself. At least, it seems that way when I listen to the words and music of the songs you've written, and read about you."

"You read about me?"

"Of course. My own daughter's been in the Branson news and you don't expect me to find out all I can? The bad thing about all this is knowing I did nothing to help you. All I did was cause you pain, and nearly destroy your life."

She closed her eyes and listened to the lap of water against the rocky shoreline below. She heard Bertie's pet goat, Mildred, bleating from somewhere past the main lodge of the bed-and-breakfast, and felt the bite of winter air on her skin.

How many times had she prayed about forgiving her father? And how often had she come away from those prayers frustrated, still overwhelmed by the inability to release her bitterness?

"I spend a lot more time in music stores

these days," he said. "I look for the names of the songwriters to see if my daughter's name is there."

She could easily recall that day at the beach when Dad had played with her and her friends in the waves…the days he'd taken her horseback riding…the nights when he wasn't drunk, when he'd stood smiling tenderly as her mom had tucked her into bed.

"You know, I'd like to meet my sister," she said at last.

"She wants to meet you, too."

"Branson's a nice place to play, especially in the winter after Christmas, when the crowds aren't so heavy."

"That sounds like an ideal setting."

She closed her eyes and breathed a quick prayer for help. Michael's words now made more sense. Forgiveness truly was a process of steps. And it was a command straight from the Bible. A person couldn't make a truth go away just because she didn't want to see it. It was like glimpsing a rattlesnake in the grass and deciding it didn't exist. The danger continued to threaten, whether she acknowledged it or not.

Lord, help me. "You could bring her," she said at last.

He didn't reply.

"Dad?"

There was a slowly indrawn breath, then "Yes." His voice sounded strained, as if by tears.

Ultimately, forgiveness was a decision, not an emotion. Grace knew that. She could make the decision now, and deal with the emotions as they came. Meanwhile she could pray about it. Jesus would be there to lead her through it.

As Grace said goodbye and disconnected, she felt a heaviness lift from her shoulders.

Maybe this hadn't turned out to be such a bad Christmas after all.

Delight pulled her Dodge Viper onto the paved driveway of Denton Mapes's elaborate stone-and-wood home, and for a moment she couldn't bring herself to get out of the car. What was she doing here?

She already had a daddy, and she loved him very much. Sure, he practically demanded perfection from her sometimes, and his rules grated, but she could always trust him to do the right thing, even if it wasn't popular. Like marrying her mom, for instance, when she carried someone else's child...and raising that child whom he loved as his own.

So what was she going to do with two fathers?

Denton stepped out the front door before she reached it.

She hadn't noticed before, but he was really a handsome man—for a father. A little dissipated, maybe, with tired bags around the eyes. Amazing how a different viewpoint could improve a person's appearance.

She wouldn't get a big head and imagine she could have any great impact on his life, but if he really was so hyped about having contact with his only child after all these years, who knew? Maybe he would be more interested in straightening a few things out, like the booze and the one-night stands.

Of course, she needed to straighten some things out, too. Wow, was Grace having an influence on her after all?

"Do I smell burning rubber?" He glanced at his watch as he stepped down from the porch. "It can't have been ten minutes since you called."

She glanced proudly over her shoulder at her car. "It gets me where I want to go."

He frowned with disapproval, and she

grinned at him. "You do the father act pretty well when you want to."

He stepped from the shade of the porch overhang, and the winter sunlight revealed streaks of white threading through his longish dark brown hair. "You spoke with your mother."

She nodded. "We had a long talk yesterday. I just flew back in this morning."

"Does that mean you're no longer afraid to come into my house?" he asked dryly.

A flush warmed her face. "You know, you should be glad I freaked. What would you have thought if I hadn't?"

He studied her soberly for a moment, and then a slow smile transformed his features.

Definitely a handsome man. For his age.

She followed him into the house and glanced up the stairway as she entered the foyer. "How many pictures do you have of me?"

"As many as I could beg from your father."

"My *father?*"

Denton gestured for her to have a seat in front of the fireplace. "He's your father, Delight. He raised you, did all the father-type things a dad does. Nothing's going to change that." He settled onto an overstuffed leather chair facing her. "I gave up trying to reach your mother and contacted your dad. We met for lunch one day, and I tried to get him to see the situation through my eyes. He did."

"So he's the one who kept you updated about me?"

Denton nodded, staring into the fire. "We've met a few times through the years. When you quit school, he called me and asked me to make sure you didn't get into trouble."

"I freaked him out when I told him about all the stuff going on at the theater."

"He wasn't happy about the direction of your career, either," Denton said, shaking his head. "He let me know about it. I don't quite get church people—all that straight-and-narrow stuff. They don't know how to have fun."

"Well, I'm still having fun, and I guess you'd say I'm one of those church people again. Anyway, I attended services last Sunday, and it felt good to be back. I also promised to start school next month. College of the Ozarks accepted me again."

"And the show?"

"It'll be a heavy load, because I'll have

to work at the college, too. Remember, it's a requirement."

He leaned back in his chair and smiled at her.

This relationship might work after all.

Grace smiled across the table at Michael. The sun rimmed a distant hillside, scattering shaded blues and purples across the surface of Table Rock Lake. The waiters raised the shades in their evening ritual at the Chateau.

"You look wonderful," Michael said.

"Thank you." This evening she'd stepped on the scales in the steamy privacy of her bathroom. She had lost twenty pounds! She still refused to wear the slinky dresses Denton wanted her to wear, and she still had some more dieting to do, but she'd learned her lesson. No more quick weight loss for her.

"Tell me something," she said. "Do you think that drug Cassidy slipped into my water might have affected my mind?"

He leaned forward. "In what way?"

"I've decided to tell Jolene what I did eight years ago. Explain why Cassidy hated me."

He nodded. "Because?"

"It's time to deal with the past," she said. "I should have done it a long time ago. People need to understand Christians aren't perfect. We make awful blunders, we sin, we struggle."

"That's true, of course, but you weren't a Christian when you did that in the first place."

"It was wrong of me to try to hide it."

"Henry told you not to talk about it."

"You and I both know I'm responsible for my own actions, not Henry or anyone else."

Michael sighed and leaned back in his chair as he gazed out at the winter sunset. "I think you're doing the right thing."

"You suggested it in the first place, remember?"

He nodded, still staring out the window. "I'm not going to miss the petty jealousies and desperate competition of this business."

She studied his features in silence as the waiter cleared their table. Disappointment pressed in on her. "You're not renewing your contract?"

He shook his head. "I'm taking some classes next semester, and I have a lot of catch-up work to do if I'm going to be a doctor someday."

"Have you decided where you're going?"

"Back to Kirksville. I've never changed my mind about osteopathy. It'll expand my options in case I want to get more into spinal manipulation someday."

"You're planning to join Cheyenne in Hideaway when you complete your training?"

He spread his hands. "Who knows? That'll be a few years. I don't want to get caught up in the medical rat race and have to fight with bureaucrats and insurance companies and attorneys. I might open my own practice on a cash-only basis."

"Then you could probably use some start-up money."

Those sultry-dark eyes focused on her. "I'm not accepting handouts, if that's what you're getting at."

"It isn't. I need some help."

His gaze didn't leave her face as he reached across the table and took her hand. "Name it."

She relished his touch. "I know you won't be signing a contract for *Star Notes,* but would you sign a contract with *me?*"

His fingers tightened on hers, and for a long moment he didn't speak. Then he gave her a teasing wink. "Grace Brennan, is that a proposal?"

She smiled. "Of a sort. You know that contract I'm supposed to sign with Dove?"

He nodded, and his grip eased. "You want me to sing with you?"

"Did you ever doubt it? We're a team, Michael. I'm not a solo act."

"You're the one they want."

"They want my songs, and they want my singing, but they're convinced now that I can't do this without the right team. To keep you from getting a big head, I've also decided to ask Blake and Delight, and Phoebe and Rachel."

He chuckled, glancing over his shoulder to beckon their waiter. "Fine. I'll sign that contract with you if you'll sign one with me."

"Did someone offer you a contract?"

"Nope."

The waiter arrived with a dessert plate, which he set in the center of their table for two. Encircling the rim of the plate were white-chocolate-dipped strawberries. In the center was a tiny but exquisitely elaborate white wedding cake topped by two sculpted white-chocolate swans in the shape of a heart. Nestled in the crook of the heart was a diamond solitaire engagement ring.

Grace caught her breath as the waiter discreetly left.

"I love you, Grace," Michael said softly.

"You already know that. I've been in agony as I've thought about moving away from here and not seeing you every day. I know you have a career to build, a true calling from God. That's why I've sacrificed so much to save my earnings so I can attend school and commute. I have a friend who will fly me from Kirksville to Branson every weekend."

"Meaning you can join us for weekend shows?"

"I think that might be arranged, but if you don't mind, I have other things to think about at the moment." He took the ring from the cake and held it out to her. "Will you marry me?"

Grace felt the tears well in her eyes and trickle down her cheeks. "Oh, Michael, I'm sorry. I'm doing it again, aren't I? We can't have a decent meal without me getting all emotional."

He laughed softly. "It's one of the things I love about you. Please don't walk out this time."

She held out her left hand. "Not a chance."

He caught and held her gaze. "No changing your mind?"

"Never. I love you. I can't imagine my life

without you in it. You're my best friend on this earth. And a whole lot more."

He placed the ring on her finger, then caught her face between his hands. She saw a promise of forever in his steadfast gaze. There was no turning back. God held their future in His hands, and she wasn't going to allow any specters from her past to interfere with her future.

Michael pulled her to him and pressed his lips to hers in the gentlest of kisses, and she felt a wave of pleasure all the way to her toes. Applause surrounded them. They looked up to find three waiters and a crowd of diners beaming at them.

Michael laughed, then caught her in his arms as if he would never let go. And she didn't want him to.

* * * * *

REQUEST YOUR FREE BOOKS!
2 FREE RIVETING INSPIRATIONAL NOVELS PLUS 2 FREE MYSTERY GIFTS

YES! Please send me 2 FREE Love Inspired® Suspense novels and my 2 FREE mystery gifts (gifts are worth about $10). After receiving them, if I don't wish to receive any more books, I can return the shipping statement marked "cancel." If I don't cancel, I will receive 4 brand-new novels every month and be billed just $4.74 per book in the U.S. or $5.24 per book in Canada. That's a savings of at least 21% off the cover price. It's quite a bargain! Shipping and handling is just 50¢ per book in the U.S. and 75¢ per book in Canada.* I understand that accepting the 2 free books and gifts places me under no obligation to buy anything. I can always return a shipment and cancel at any time. Even if I never buy another book, the two free books and gifts are mine to keep forever.

123/323 IDN F5AN

Name	(PLEASE PRINT)
Address	Apt. #
City	State/Prov.	Zip/Postal Code

Signature (if under 18, a parent or guardian must sign)

Mail to the Harlequin® Reader Service:
IN U.S.A.: P.O. Box 1867, Buffalo, NY 14240-1867
IN CANADA: P.O. Box 609, Fort Erie, Ontario L2A 5X3

Are you a current subscriber to Love Inspired Suspense books and want to receive the larger-print edition? Call 1-800-873-8635 or visit www.ReaderService.com.

* Terms and prices subject to change without notice. Prices do not include applicable taxes. Sales tax applicable in N.Y. Canadian residents will be charged applicable taxes. Offer not valid in Quebec. This offer is limited to one order per household. Not valid for current subscribers to Love Inspired Suspense books. All orders subject to credit approval. Credit or debit balances in a customer's account(s) may be offset by any other outstanding balance owed by or to the customer. Please allow 4 to 6 weeks for delivery. Offer available while quantities last.

LISDIR13R

REQUEST YOUR FREE BOOKS!

2 FREE INSPIRATIONAL NOVELS
PLUS 2
FREE
MYSTERY GIFTS

Love Inspired
HISTORICAL
INSPIRATIONAL HISTORICAL ROMANCE

YES! Please send me 2 FREE Love Inspired® Historical novels and my 2 FREE mystery gifts (gifts are worth about $10). After receiving them, if I don't wish to receive any more books, I can return the shipping statement marked "cancel." If I don't cancel, I will receive 4 brand-new novels every month and be billed just $4.74 per book in the U.S. or $5.24 per book in Canada. That's a savings of at least 21% off the cover price. It's quite a bargain! Shipping and handling is just 50¢ per book in the U.S. and 75¢ per book in Canada.* I understand that accepting the 2 free books and gifts places me under no obligation to buy anything. I can always return a shipment and cancel at any time. Even if I never buy another book, the two free books and gifts are mine to keep forever.

102/302 IDN F5CY

Name	(PLEASE PRINT)
Address	Apt. #
City	State/Prov.	Zip/Postal Code

Signature (if under 18, a parent or guardian must sign)

Mail to the **Harlequin® Reader Service:**
IN U.S.A.: P.O. Box 1867, Buffalo, NY 14240-1867
IN CANADA: P.O. Box 609, Fort Erie, Ontario L2A 5X3

Want to try two free books from another series?
Call 1-800-873-8635 or visit www.ReaderService.com.

* Terms and prices subject to change without notice. Prices do not include applicable taxes. Sales tax applicable in N.Y. Canadian residents will be charged applicable taxes. Offer not valid in Quebec. This offer is limited to one order per household. Not valid for current subscribers to Love Inspired Historical books. All orders subject to credit approval. Credit or debit balances in a customer's account(s) may be offset by any other outstanding balance owed by or to the customer. Please allow 4 to 6 weeks for delivery. Offer available while quantities last.

Your Privacy—The Harlequin® Reader Service is committed to protecting your privacy. Our Privacy Policy is available online at www.ReaderService.com or upon request from the Harlequin Reader Service.

We make a portion of our mailing list available to reputable third parties that offer products we believe may interest you. If you prefer that we not exchange your name with third parties, or if you wish to clarify or modify your communication preferences, please visit us at www.ReaderService.com/consumerschoice or write to us at Harlequin Reader Service Preference Service, P.O. Box 9062, Buffalo, NY 14269. Include your complete name and address.

LIHDIR13R

Reader Service.com

Manage your account online!
- Review your order history
- Manage your payments
- Update your address

> ### *We've designed the Harlequin® Reader Service website just for you.*

Enjoy all the features!
- Reader excerpts from any series
- Respond to mailings and special monthly offers
- Discover new series available to you
- Browse the Bonus Bucks catalog
- Share your feedback

Visit us at:
ReaderService.com